I0668850

ZEPPELINS OVER AFRIKA

Airship 27 Productions

Zeppelins Over Afrika
© 2022 Gene Moyers

Published by Airship 27 Productions
www.airship27.com
www.airship27hangar.com

Interior illustrations © 2022 Mike Harris
Cover illustration © 2022 Brian McCulloch

Editor: Ron Fortier
Associate Editor: Jay Sweet
Marketing and Promotions Manager: Michael Vance
Production designer: Rob Davis

ISBN: 978-1-953589-38-5

Printed in the United States of America

10 9 8 7 6 5 4 3 2 1

BY GENE MOYERS

*The story **Flight of the Wasp** was published earlier in a slightly different form by Pro Se Press. Special thanks goes out to Tommy Hancock for giving me the impetus to write my first Zeppelin story.*

TIMELINE

1896 Aviation pioneer Otto Lillienthal killed while testing his manned glider.

1898 1st Flight of Count Von Zeppelin's LZ-1 is moderately successful.

1899 Aviation glider developer Percy Pilcher killed while testing his glider.

1st Flight of LZ-2 is a successful 6-hour flight.

1900 LZ-3 flies for hours over German cities to great acclaim. The Zeppelin is later destroyed at its moorings due to a sudden storm. German citizens contribute millions of Marks to a rebuilding effort. Reichstag aid is given.

1901 LZ-4 and LZ-5 are flown successfully.

1902 Zeppelin Stiftung (foundation) formed. LZ-6 flown.

1903 DELAG formed by Count Von Zeppelin and Hugo Eckener to fly commercial Zeppelins linking German cities.

Wilbur Wright is killed at Kittyhawk North Carolina testing the Wright Flyer. Orville Wright abandons flight attempts and returns to live in seclusion in Ohio.

1904 German Navy takes possession of its first Zeppelin. DELAG establishes commercial service to London, Paris and other western European cities.

1905 Both Britain and France announce ambitious airship programs. Both programs progress slowly and are less than successful.

1907 DELAG has flown a quarter million miles. There is service now to all parts of Western Europe, Greece, Turkey and Egypt. Heavier than air development has essentially been abandoned. European engine manufacturers concentrate on large, heavy, water cooled diesel engines geared for large, slow paddle type propellers to sell to airship manufacturers. Light weight, air cooled, high rpm engines are not developed to their potential.

1908 German Navy is now flying a dozen Zeppelins. The American Navy purchases a Zeppelin from Germany. Russia belatedly announces an ambitious airship program but it is continually delayed due to poor economic conditions in Russia as well as lack of technical expertise.

1909 Both France and Britain are flying a few airships but they are technically primitive compared to Germany's Zeppelins. Several accidents occur. German Navy sends two Zeppelins on a tour of their African colonies. One Zeppelin has a minor landing accident in German Southwest Africa and is

5

delayed for repairs by one month. Otherwise the flight is a triumph.

1910 DELAG begins commercial service to German African colonies, especially German East Africa (DOA). This stimulates commercial and military development of the DOA. Emigration to Africa increases quickly.

1914 War breaks out in Europe in the Fall. Germany, Austria and a few minor allies are allied against Britain, France and Russia. Germany has over fifty military Zeppelins available. More civilian Zeppelins are pressed into service. France and Britain have less than a dozen airships between them and they are not tactically effective. Spearheaded by their massive fleet of Zeppelins, Germany attacks through Belgium into France. Northeastern France is quickly occupied and Paris surrounded. A front is finally established running from Caen to Dijon. Russia is active against Austria, while they are defeated in a series of large battles in the east against German forces. The few German Zeppelins there give Germany a big advantage.

1915 Paris falls after six months of siege. British forces evacuate LeHavre. Numerous ship actions are fought in or near the English Channel. Both side suffer heavy losses. Unrestricted German submarine warfare takes an alarming toll on Allied shipping. A series of major but ultimately indecisive fleet actions are fought in the North Sea. Zeppelins give the Germans the advantage. The rebuilt French Government attempts to negotiate terms. Russian gradually loses ground against Germany. Austria suffers alarming casualties but stays in the war. Strategic Zeppelin Bombing of Britain takes its toll on morale. German Togoland and German Southwest Africa are occupied. Heavy fighting occurs in the DOA.

1915 Spring: France signs a separate peace treaty with Germany. British diversionary campaigns in Africa are slowed due to lack of troops from Europe and strategic intervention by Zeppelins. Worried about Europe and upset about submarine warfare America leans toward war on the Allied side. A vote is scheduled in the late Spring. Italy prepares to enter the war against Austria but rethinks this after a mysterious suspension of commercial Zeppelin traffic due to "technical difficulties" as well as a massive demonstration of German Airpower around their shores. In early May Germany launches thirty Zeppelins deep into Russia and attack the Summer Palace. Carrying nearly three thousand troops they capture the Czar and royal family. Britain vows to fight on but public opinion is turning against the war. In Russia the Duma meets to pick a new Czar from the Romanov family. Civil War breaks out and the Duma flees. Russian forces request a cease fire with Germany. In Washington on the eve of a congressional vote, news of the Russian debacle arrives and the vote is cancelled. America stays neutral. Britain reluctantly decides to open negotiations with Germany. Japan attacks German colonies in China and the Pacific (The Marshall Islands) without a declaration of war.

1915 Summer In the peace treaty France permanently recognizes German ownership of Alsace and Lorraine. It also withdraws its troops from German Cameroons and agrees to give up its colony of Martinique. Germany returns the Tsar to Russia and aids it against insurgencies. Britain withdraws from all German territories. Germany withdraws to prewar borders. Belgium is returned to prewar borders and reparations are paid by Germany. Japan refuses to attend any peace negotiations. Ominously Germany says nothing about Japan. As nations are moving forces and demobilizing, Polish rebels revolt in eastern Germany and western Russia. Germany suppresses its rebels but stays neutral as Russia attempts to suppress the Polish armies.

1915 Fall After a short series of bloody engagements Polish forces are finally destroyed but restive Poles remain a thorn in Russia's side. Germany organizes a very large "Peace Tour" by its battle fleet. Accompanying this fleet are more than two dozen Zeppelins supported by several Zeppelin passenger ships converted into "Zeppelin Tenders." The fleet is also accompanied by troop ships carrying thousands of battle tested troops. Traveling via South America they sail for the Marshall Islands and retake them against token opposition. Several Japanese warships mysteriously disappear during this process. As the fleet appears near Okinawa they are met by Japanese government officials at sea. Negotiations take place quickly. The Marshalls are recognized as German. Japan flatly refuses to return Tsingtao to Germany and instead pays a huge indemnity for it. Deciding against a distant war Germany accepts the situation but relations are forever strained with Japan.

1915-1920 France and Russia are the biggest losers of "The Great War." Germany is a big winner. Her Zeppelins and command of the air won the war for her. England loses no territory but her losses in men and equipment rank close to Russia and France. Warship losses are serious. France is nearly bankrupt and must rebuild. Britain undergoes an economic recession and cuts military expenditures. Russia is in chaos fighting insurrections and bankrupt, propped up only by German and American loans to the Tsar's government. Germany spent huge amounts of money during the war. Its losses in ships and men are heavy but an economic expansion takes place in her African colonies. Many people emigrate especially to DOA. Emboldened by their long-range use of Zeppelins, DELAG initiates commercial service to North and South America. This expansion pays their war debts, and more. Careful observers of the war, American studies German Zeppelins and enter into an agreement with the Germans to help build several large modern airships for their navy. In exchange the Americans agree to sell helium to the Germans.

1920-1930 Gradually Europe settles into a cold war. Britain and France, along with Belgium and some minor allies resent and fear Germany. Austria gains nothing from the war and limps along attempting to pay its debts while trading on its alliance with Germany. Russian forces finally regain a measure of control inside their borders but spend years putting down communist insurgencies and various nationalist revolts. Turkey, although neutral, during the war begins to collapse economically as it too fights a series of revolts from Arabs, Yemenis and Kurds, often aided covertly by a Persia that is expanding in the Persian Gulf. Italy, Spain and Portugal remain neutral, their loyalties shifting with every European Crisis. With this "Cold War" come incidents. There are numerous border skirmishes and incursions, mysterious ship disappearances and outright naval battles between the European powers. Britain lets its battle fleet drop to parity with Germany but modernizes and increases its cruiser force, especially overseas. Germany concentrates on improving its cruiser force and building up its African colonies. A new naval base is established on the Rufiji River. Dar Es Salaam is built up and permanent naval forces are stationed in the DOA. Three permanent airship stations are built at Tabora, Dar Es Salaam and on the Rufiji River. In the Pacific, Germany is at odds with the other European powers. Everyone is suspicious of Japan. America is again neutral with everyone except an expansionist Japan which it distrusts. Tens of thousands of Germans emigrate to their colonies, especially DOA causing massive development there. During all this America grows rich selling oil, steel, aluminum, copper and helium to anyone who will buy it.

1935 America is recovering from an economic disruption that affected Europe much less. Germany is doing well and bridging a series of new weapons on line; K class cruisers, Battle cruisers, the new "colonial" cruisers, armored cars, tanks and the new experimental paratroopers. With heavier than air flight still born, the only serious flying is done in airships, although small scale private experiments with heavier than air craft continue. Germany has the biggest fleet of airships. American ships, based on proven German designs, are excellent but she has a smaller fleet than Germany to scout for her navy. The British new R-80 class ships are very good designs but are just coming online. French airships aren't particularly effective. They refuse to buy British airships due to national pride. Many neutral powers buy German civilian airships although America is beginning to sell significant numbers of commercial Goodyear airships. Britain and France are jealous of Germany and determined to chip away at her African colonies. Without consulting France, Britain has decided on a lightning campaign to occupy German Togoland. Diversionary attacks in other German colonies will hopefully slow or deter German retaliation.

PROLOGUE

1935

It has been over twenty years since Germany won the Great European War. At that time the major European powers were divided into complicated defense alliances; France, Russia and Great Britain in the Triple Entente and Germany, Austria-Hungary and Italy in the Triple Alliance. When Austria's squabbles with Serbia erupted in war in the fall of 1914, Russia mobilized against Austria to protect her Slavic ally. Germany then honored her commitments and declared war against Russia. A cascade of mobilizations followed immediately and Europe quickly found itself at war.

While Russia mobilized its vast reserves, Austria began attacks in southeastern Europe. Germany meanwhile implemented a long-planned offensive in the west and invaded France via Belgium. Marching around the clock and led by her mighty Zeppelin fleet, German forces ignored and bypassed Belgian cities and quickly marched into northern France. Zeppelins dropped forces that took and held strategic bridges, road junctions and towns. They also bombed French forces as they mobilized and moved to the front. England attempted to land an expeditionary force to help her French ally but was frustrated by German bombing. Calais, Dunkirk and Boulogne quickly fell just as British transports arrived. The British attempted a landing at Dieppe but were forced to withdraw by round the clock Zeppelin bombings. They were finally able to get ashore in force at Le Havre but were slowed by bombing and eventually bottled up by fast moving German ground forces.

The French were hard pressed to set up defensive lines. With over fifty Zeppelins to support their forces there were always airships overhead to scout for the German columns. If French forces were spotted, the Zeppelins merely guided German forces around them forcing the French to withdraw. If the French began to deploy defensive lines German Zeppelins bombed them mercilessly. With no airships of its own and no effective anti-aircraft guns, French forces were never able to build a continuous defense line.

Within five weeks of the start of offensive actions the German army was closing in on Paris. The Belgian army had retreated into the north of their country to protect Brussels and Antwerp. The Germans made no

9

attacks in Belgium and instead proffered "cease fire in place" feelers. The French government refused to abandon their capital and the Germans surrounded Paris and declared a siege seven weeks into the campaign.

The French finally managed to set up a continuous line of defense running roughly from Caen through Orleans to Dijon. German forces halted at that point and let the French dig in. They concentrated instead on the sieges of LeHavre and Paris. For the next two months German naval forces fought a series of battles with the Grand Fleet in the English Channel and its eastern approaches that threatened the British foothold in France. Naval casualties were heavy on both sides. Finally the British withdrew their battered expeditionary forces from LeHavre, and it fell days later.

Paris continued to hold out as the French carried out a series of massive attacks attempting to relieve the city. From behind their trench lines, the German were ready for every French attack due to their command of aerial reconnaissance. Barbed wire, artillery and emplaced machine guns did the rest. After six months of siege Paris surrendered to Imperial German forces. Reluctantly, what was left of the French government sued for a ceasefire.

After a typically slow mobilization, Russia had put its large armies into action on the eastern front. Poorly supplied and poorly led, the Russians were largely repulsed in a series of battles in East Prussia with German forces fighting mainly defensive battles. Early in this campaign the Germans inflicted a stinging defeat on the Russians at the Battle of Tannenberg. The Russians had more success against the Austrians but front lines did not change much in the first eight months of the war.

With a shaky ceasefire in place in the west and negotiations ongoing, German forces shifted massive forces eastward in the spring of 1915. The Germans transferred over thirty Zeppelins to the eastern front. This allowed large scale German offensive moves. The remainder of her Zeppelins remained in the west and continued their bombardment of England.

German intelligence had kept a close eye on the Tsar Nichols II's movements and when the time was right they struck. A raiding force of nearly thirty Zeppelins loaded with battle tested German troops penetrated deep into Russia and landed three thousand troops to surround the summer palace of the Tsar. He was guarded by significant numbers of Imperial Guards troops but after hours of fierce battle the Tsar was captured and returned to Germany as a prisoner along with his family. At the cost of eight Zeppelins and a few hundred casualties the Germans had changed the course of the war in the east.

News of this coup spread like wild fire all across Europe. It helped convince French negotiators to come to terms and a peace treaty between France and Germany was signed within two weeks of the Tsar's capture. Germany then concluded negotiations with Belgium on very liberal terms. They even offered to pay reparations for property damaged in their march through to France.

Stubbornly Britain fought on. They ignored German peace feelers and continued their attacks on German colonies in Africa. They conquered Togoland, and most of German Southwest Africa but found the going much harder in German East Africa. There German settlers and their well-trained Askaris supplied by Zeppelins put up a hard fight. The British also sortied into the North Sea and fought a huge fleet battle with the German High Seas Fleet. Losses were high on both sides before battle was broken off by a German retreat.

Meanwhile Russia had descended into chaos after the Tsar's capture. Rival governments had been declared by Republican forces and by Communists under Lenin. With France knocked out of the war and Russia torn by civil conflict British morale plummeted and public opinion turned against the war.

Concerned about German domination of the continent the American Congress began debates about entering the war on the British side. Unrestrained German submarine warfare had inflamed American sensibilities and the public seemed favorable to this. A congressional vote was postponed and then canceled as Britain agreed to peace negotiations. Effectively, in less than a year of war the German Empire had shifted the balance of power in Europe.

Negotiations went quickly. The main concessions the British made the return of all Germany's overseas colonies. All combatants agreed to pay for their own losses with the exception of Germany to Belgium. European frontiers were generally restored to prewar boundaries. The main result of the war was that now Germany dominated European land politics. This was finalized by her restoration of the Russian monarchy and assistance in putting down the Russian revolts. The only permanent loss the Germans suffered was their Far Eastern colony in China which the Japanese occupied without a declaration of war. After hostilities were over Japan steadfastly refuse to return Tsingtao to Germany earning them a top spot on the Emperor's enemy list.

After the war, Germany quickly re-tooled her Zeppelin production to civilian airships. Zeppelin transport to European cities was expanded and soon the Zeps began ranging across the Atlantic. The *American Goodyear Corporation* quickly formed a joint company with the Zeppelin Works to form the *Goodyear Zeppelin Corporation* and was soon producing German designed airships for American forces. Gradually Europe settled into a period of armed neutrality that came to be known as the "Cold War" that has lasted for more than two decades. Europe is a cauldron of old rivalries, shifting alliances, nationalistic ambitions and intrigue. The major powers exist in a state of uneasy peace that threatens to break out into open conflict at any time.

In Russia the Tsar now sits on his throne courtesy of the German Emperor. After the Tsar was returned to his throne, German troops helped restore order. Revolts led by nationalists under Kerensky and Communists under Lenin were put down. Lenin was captured and executed. Kerensky fled into exile and a weak Russian monarchy was restored. Today the Tsar's nation is plagued by ethnic revolts and nationalistic plots.

France has rebuilt its army and increased the size of its fleet. It longs for revenge against Germany but knows it is no match for its neighbor. It settles for making trouble overseas whenever it can. Particularly bitter to the French was the forced surrender of the island of Martinique to the German Empire.

England stung by a series of expensive sea battles with the German High Seas Fleet and embarrassed by withdrawal of its French expeditionary force saw its peace with Germany as a stain on national honor. Although England agreed to a restoration of the pre-war borders, including the return of all German territory in Africa, it has never been happy with the treaty. It maintains a large fleet to deter German aggression in Europe and significant ground forces in Africa. It too looks for any opening to chip away at German power.

Austria-Hungary survived the war intact, but suffered heavy casualties fighting off Russian attacks in southeast Europe. Since the war its restive minorities have been its main preoccupation. Political crises and independence movements are a constant problem. It has slid to minor power status in Europe.

Turkey remains the "Sick Man of Europe." Although avoiding participation in the war, it has its hands full dealing with revolts in its Middle Eastern provinces. Similar to Russia's situation, it is in danger of breaking apart at any moment.

Italy avoided the war. A revolution in 1922 brought the dictator Mussolini to power. It has pretensions to be a major power but it lacks sufficient finances and an economic base. Its military is fairly weak.

Spain has maintained questionable neutrality for many years. Its loyalty shifts constantly with the political situation. Internally plagued by political instability during the twenties it has stabilized in the last few years as a nominal monarchy backed by a powerful military junta. It maintains a small army and fleet in Europe but significant forces in its North African colonies.

Portugal, never a major power in Europe, maintains strong forces in its African colonies. It, like Spain, shifts its alliances as it sees fit and the political situation dictates

Germany is now the most powerful country in Europe but must remain constantly on guard against its neighbors. It maintains a large naval fleet in European waters to balance the British fleet. Its large army is a threat that keeps the peace in Europe. It has poured many resources into its returned African colonies and they are not only successful but quite profitable. Its large Zeppelin fleet, both civilian and military, fly huge airships fantastic distances. Passenger and mail service connects Germany with North and South America. Regular Zeppelin flights expedite communication between Germany and its overseas colonies.

Barely avoiding participation in the Great War, America generally maintains neutrality in its relations with the European powers. Safe behind two wide oceans, it guards its neutrality with strong surface fleets aided by squadrons of powerful naval airships. Its long-standing alliance with *DELAG* and the Zeppelin company have assured that its airships are as good as Germany's and a qualitative step ahead of those flown by France and Great Britain. Meanwhile America grows rich selling oil, steel, aluminum and above all helium to the rival European powers.

While Europe enjoys an uneasy peace, conflict goes on elsewhere. The high seas are unsafe. Warships are on alert and lonely sea battles are fought on distant oceans. Merchant ships are stopped and searched without warning. Ships go missing and are never seen again. Are they victims of, unknown raiders, hostile submarines or floating mines of unknown origin?

The seas are dangerous but by far the biggest area of competition is Africa. Nearly the entire continent is still controlled by various European powers. In these colonies, far from media scrutiny and government oversight, conflict is rampant. Border incidents, rebel forces supported by enemy governments and brush fire wars are common. Afraid of an apocalyptic war at home, Africa serves as a proxy arena for conflict amongst the European powers. Most maintain large colonial armies, naval bases and warships in their colonies.

By far the large colonial powers of France, Germany and Great Britain dominate African affairs but Spain, Italy, Belgium and Portugal keep a close eye on their colonial possessions. Recent months have been somewhat stable in Africa but Great Britain has decided the time is right to shift the African playing field in its favor while giving its old rival Germany a bloody nose. It has carefully massed ships and troops in West Africa and is prepared to present Germany with a startling "fait accompli." As the morning sun rises over East Africa, hostilities are imminent.

PART ONE

FLIGHT OF THE WASP

Oberleutnant zur See Max Von Clausen stepped out of the officer's quarters into the blinding Africa sun. It was early morning in Tabora and the sun was still low in the east. The morning temperature was pleasant but Max knew that soon it would rise with the sun. He had only been in Africa two weeks and was still adjusting to the climate. It was a far cry from his home in Bavaria. There, November would have brought a chill to the air and people would be wearing warm clothes preparing for winter. Here in the German East Africa it was hot and dry although the short rainy season was just weeks away.

The trim, twenty-one-year-old officer turned to look at the huge silver shape that dominated the airfield. A light breeze stirred his short brown hair. The Zeppelin L-107 was one of two permanently assigned airships here in the DOA (Deutsche Ost Afrika or German East Africa in English.) Max was assigned as navigator for the great airship. Although experienced flying in Zeppelins this was his first overseas posting. He was becoming familiar with the routine and his new crewmates but was a bit intimidated by his new commanding officer.

Even now as he crossed, he could see the tall form of Korvetten Kapitan Walter Trautloff standing in the shadow cast by the enormous airship accepting something from an enlisted man. The naval rating saluted and left. As he neared his commander, Max could see him reading a message of some sort. He approached and saluted. Trautloff ignored the salute. Finally, he turned and handed the paper to Max. The flimsy radio office form read:

From: Commander German Naval Airship Division
To: All Naval Airship Commands

At 0500 hours local time naval and land forces of Great Britain invaded German Togoland. Local forces have resisted and casualties have occurred. This is to be considered a war alert to all Imperial German Afrikan forces. All Afrikan units are permitted to take all defensive and offensive actions to protect Imperial citizens and property.

Signed: Flottenadmiral Johannes Hoffman

Max looked up in confusion. Trautloff's face was impassive as he handed Max another radio message. He saw that it was dated just minutes before:

From: Commander SMS Gazelle
To: Commander Naval forces East Afrika.

This command attacked at dawn by large enemy warship flying flag of Great Britain.
Ship is unknown to this command. Enemy is heavily armed and we have taken serious damage and casualties. Am retiring south. Request immediate assistance and air cover.
Position approx. 150km SW of Kisumu.

Max felt a chill despite the warm African air. He looked at Trautloff who seemed calm as he took back the messages and said, "Better get aboard Leutnant, we lift off in ten minutes." Max saluted and turned toward the boarding ladder hanging from the control cabin. He turned back as Trautloff spoke again, "Chart an intercepting course to *Gazelle's* position." As Max nodded and scrambled up the ladder into the cabin, the air raid siren mounted atop the tall mooring mast began to sound.

Within minutes the giant airship was ready to launch. Her twenty-eight crewmen were at their stations. The six powerful engines idled and the ground crew stood ready at the landing ropes. The captain gave the command to release from the mooring mast and the ground crew kept a taut hold on the ground lines as the Zeppelin gradually turned into the light wind. When all was ready Captain Trautloff gave the command, "Schiff Hoch!" The lines were let go and the Zeppelin slid gracefully into the sky.

Trautloff looked expectantly at Max who called out confidently, "Course 015 degrees, sir." Trautloff nodded and gave the order to the bridge crew; the two helmsmen repeated the orders. Looking forward Max could see them standing at right angles to each other. One facing forward in the nose of the control car to work the rudder control wheel, and one facing to port controlling another large wheel connected the giant elevators mounted on the horizontal tail fins. Max's navigating table was near the middle of the car across from the wireless room.

As he was marking the course and times in the log the captain appeared at his shoulder, "What is the time to *Gazelle's* last known position?"

Max looked up, "Approximately 3 hours thirty minutes at 130 kilometers per hour, sir. This will be shorter if she continues south toward us."

The captain nodded. "If she's still afloat."

A few minutes later the first officer climbed down the ladder to the hull onto the control deck. He conferred briefly with the captain and then they both turned toward the navigating table. As Kapitan Leutnant Peter Wenig looked over their projected course the captain asked him, "What's the bomb load, Peter?"

Without looking up Wenig replied, "Fifty 50-kilogram bombs, eighteen 100-kilogram bombs and 100 kilograms of incendiaries."

The captain looked thoughtful. "I wish we'd had time to swap everything out for more 50s."

Max's comment was out before he realized it. "The 100-kilogram bombs will be more effective against a ship, sir. They have nearly as much destructive power as a shell from one of our heavy cruisers. Two or three hits might be enough to disable it." He looked confident. The first officer smiled and looked away.

The captain's face remained impassive as his eyes bored into Max's. "You've been in the Naval air Service for two years haven't you Lieutnant?"

"Yes, sir."

"Your record says you had high scores in both navigation and bombard-ment."

...his eyes bored into Max's.

"Yes, sir."

"Then you have had training in the North Sea attacking moving targets and know how difficult it is?"

Max hesitated. He could feel his face warming as he replied. "Yes, sir but when I was on L-92 we scored nearly ten percent hits on a moving target, surely…"

"A towed target moving at what? Ten knots, from fifteen hundred meters?"

"Well, uh yes, sir."

"Son, attacking a fast-moving warship while it's firing and forcing you to higher altitudes is another matter altogether. We'll have to drop salvoes and hope we get lucky. The more bombs, the better a chance of a hit."

Max's face turned red as he nodded. Although he had been in the navy for nearly four years, and in the Naval Air Service for over two he had not seen combat. The captain turned to his first officer. "What about this ship? Do you think she has heavy flak guns?"

Wenig shrugged. "The British have kept her building a secret; our spies have reported nothing about her. She must be powerful though; *Antelope* and *Gazelle* are the strongest warships on Lake Victoria…or at least they were."

The captain nodded. "Perhaps we can get more information from *Gazelle* as we get closer." He nodded to the two officers and returned to the front of the car. Max looked expectantly at Wenig.

The first officer shook his head. "We have to hope she doesn't have heavy flak guns. We'll have little chance of scoring hits if we're forced above 3,000 meters." Max thoughtfully went back to his charts.

The African veldt unrolled below them. It was a beautiful day and Max spent as much time as he could looking out at the scenery below. The control car was built into the body of the Zeppelin in the lower nose of the ship and afforded a spectacular view ahead. He kept his mind on his job though, watching his charts and matching them to visible landmarks.

He approached the captain at the two-hour mark. "Sir, we should be sighting Lake Victoria soon, off the port bow." The captain nodded without taking his eyes from his binoculars. Within minutes there was a buzz. The captain grabbed the intercom handset off the bulkhead, listened for a moment, thanked whoever it was and hung up. He spoke aloud, "Forward lookout sights water bearing 330."

Max smiled. At this point there was a long bay in Lake Victoria's southern shore that led to Germany's main port on the lake, Mwansa.

They would pass just to the east of it. Soon he could see the full expanse of the Lake filling the forward port as they passed over Mwansa and out over Lake Victoria. The captain asked for the time to their destination.

Max glanced quickly at his chart and replied, "ETA to Gazelle's last reported position in approximately one hour fifteen minutes, sir."

A half hour later the intercom buzzed again. After taking the call from the forward lookout, the captain announced a ship sighted ahead. Soon they could see smoke on the horizon from the control car. The captain conned his ship toward it and soon they were circling over the warship.

Max had seen battle-damaged ships before but he was still shocked at SMS Gazelle's appearance. She was a thousand-ton steamer, shorter than a destroyer but wider. She was armed with 105mm guns fore and aft and many smaller weapons. Passing over the warship at 600 meters Max could see she had been hard hit. Smoke still spiraled up from her stern. He could see twisted wreckage and actual holes in the side of the ship. Her forward gun appeared totally destroyed.

At this time the wireless began clicking. The captain took the message from the radio operator. He read it and spoke aloud, "Gazelle was hit hard but is not in danger of sinking. Her engines were not damaged and she finally out ran the enemy. They broke contact over an hour ago. Enemy last seen heading northeast." He moved to the chart and ran his finger across it, "They're probably heading back to Kisumu. Lieutnant, give me a course and ETA."

Max jumped to his table and soon had the information. He gave the captain his course recommendation and the captain gave the orders. Soon they turned northeast.

An hour later they were cutting across a few miles of headland to enter the deep bay that led to the British port of Kisumu. As they crossed back over the lake smoke was again sighted. This time the captain called the crew to battle stations and ordered a climb to 2,000 meters. As they neared the enemy Max got a look at it through his binoculars. The ship was a large steamer and flew the British flag. She was armed with at least two large guns forward and two aft. A large crew scrambled about the decks. Once over the enemy, tracers began to reach up from the ship.

Max tensed even though he knew the tracers were from light machine guns that couldn't reach them. Then several small dark puffs appeared several hundred meters below them. He could feel the captain relax next to him.

The captain lowered his binoculars and turned to Max. "Well, it looks like they have only light flak guns aboard. Those are probably old one-pounders, or maybe two-pounders. If they had the new ones they might be able to reach us." He turned to the steersmen and ordered, "Bring us in behind the enemy. Make your altitude 1800 meters."

Max moved to the rear of the car just forward of the rear gunner's position and uncovered the large and cumbersome bombsight. The captain replaced the handset and moved to stand next to Max who looked up from the sight and questioned, "What do you think the target's speed is, sir?"

The captain replied, "Let's find out." He turned and barked out. "Engines three and four to idle. Conform to the target's speed."

Max set the height and looked through the sight but his field of view was narrow and all he could see was water. He waited, his palms growing damp as the captain gave more orders to bring the airship above and behind the warship.

Finally, Max looked up. The captain was staring at the gauges in the steering compartment. He looked back at Max and called out, "Target is doing about fourteen knots." He did a quick mental calculation and added, "Set your target speed at twenty-six kilometers per hour."

Max called back confirmation and dialed in their speed. He looked through the sight as the target drifted into his range of vision.

Here was where he earned his money.

Max called out small course corrections until gradually the target steadied in his sight. He thought of the sailors below watching helplessly as the huge airship loomed above them. They would have to wait for the bombs to fall away toward them before they could attempt to evade.

Max, called out, "Stand by!" When the ship settled squarely in the crosshairs Max yelled, "Drop!"

The captain had the intercom handset to his head and repeated Max's command. Max continued to look through his sight. Ten seconds passed. Fifteen seconds. Twenty seconds; and then Max saw the ship below him turning to starboard. Slow at first and then faster. As it moved to the edge of his vision he jumped up and scrambled to a port. The enemy ship was turning faster now. Then the bombs hit the water.

They were too high to hear the explosions but each bomb threw up a huge waterspout. The explosions came in a rapid string, taking no more than three seconds. They were strung out in a rough pattern moving toward the ship. Max held his breath as the white fountains of water neared their target but he was disappointed. The final bomb fell probably within fifteen meters of the ship, but that was as close as they came.

Max gritted his teeth. He was sure they would get at least one hit. He moved back to his sight as the captain calmly gave orders. The airship turned to circle around once more behind their target.

The captain was at his side a moment later. "I'm going to bring us own to 1,600 meters. That's as low as I can go. We'll give them twenty more 50 kgs. What's the fall time from there?"

Max did some quick mathematics in his head and replied, "Uh, forty to forty-five seconds, sir."

The captain shook his head, "Let's hope we get lucky." He returned to the front of the control cabin to line up the attack. Max dialed in the new height. Within a few minutes they were behind the enemy, matching speeds as before. As Max bent over his sight the ship was buffeted gently. He called out a minor course correction. The ship moved into his sight as the Zeppelin was buffeted again.

He was about to call for steadiness on the helm when there was a bang. Max jerked his head up. Wind whistled through a jagged hole near his right foot. The ship was jolted again and he realized the jolting was from flak exploding just below them. He gulped and pushed his face back down on the sight, calling out course corrections as the Zeppelin jolted about.

Gradually the enemy ship steadied in his crosshairs. When it did, he sang out. "Drop!" The captain repeated the command. Max again scrambled over to the port.

Max didn't see the bombs as they fell but he saw the blossoms of water as they exploded. Unfortunately, none of them hit. The ship had commenced a sharp turn as soon as they saw the bombs. They had less time to maneuver but still avoided all the falling bombs, although the last one exploded so close the ship was showered with water. Max felt his temper rising. Dozens of bombs and none of them had hit! He turned back to his sight in time to hear the captain ordering the engines to full and a course northeast.

He was shocked. He went forward to ask, "Herr Kapitan, we're breaking off the attack?"

The captain turned to him. "Another attack will do no good, Leutnant. We cannot go any lower without risking serious damage. We have other business."

Max turned away disappointed as the captain began calling for damage reports. He went to his charts and began calculations. Kisumu was only a half hour away at full speed. He passed this information to the captain.

Soon enough they were over the British port. It wasn't a large town and was dominated by the docks. As they cruised over them at 1,800 meters the captain pointed out a large dockside building that seemed to have no roof. That particular building had once been a factory for canning fish. It must have been secretly turned into a dock for modifying and arming the enemy warship. As they cruised over the town they started receiving enemy fire. Most of the flak burst below them but there were a few stray larger bursts that were near their altitude.

They turned and set up for a bomb run against the docks. With his altitude and speed set, Max watched through his sight as the docks appeared. He sang out when the first long pier entered his vision. The captain began calling off bomb releases. They used the larger 100-kilogram bombs this time, releasing them in sequence as they sailed over the waterfront. When they had cleared the harbor they turned and made another run. This time they emptied their bomb racks and their incendiaries as well. When they left the area all the piers were in flames, as was every boat and ship moored there.

As they turned south for home the captain commented. "We've missed the ship but we'll have other chances. Meanwhile she won't have a base to return to any time soon." There were a few nods at this but Max was still chagrined that he hadn't gotten even one hit. There had to be a better way.

At eleven the next morning Max knocked at the captain's office door. It had been a long night. They had fought headwinds all the way back to Tabora and had not moored until sunset. But that wasn't the end of Max's day. He had accompanied the captain throughout the ship. He had spoken to every crewmember and checked all damage himself. He had insisted that Max come along to familiarize himself with the crew and ship.

The captain had eventually gone off to a conference with senior staff. Max had spent most of the rest of the night helping Leutnant Wenig see to repairs and provisioning. Helping lift bombs into their racks had been back breaking work and Max had finally tumbled into bed fully dressed at three in the morning after jerking off his boots.

A shower and change of uniform had brought him semi-alert as he entered the office. The captain was pointing at a large map of eastern Africa on the wall while the first officer listened. They turned as Max entered the office, his cap under one arm.

"Ah, Max, I was just passing on what I learned at last night's briefing."

Leutnant Wenig nodded to Max as he moved up to listen. "So, the High Command is not expecting a full-scale invasion here but they do expect major thrusts to keep us distracted from Togoland."

Wenig stroked his chin thoughtfully. "By sea, Herr Kapitan?"

"Probably. The East Afrika squadron has put to sea from our Rufiji base. They are cruising off Mafia Island now. L-102 is scouting for them. Sea defenses are on alert at Tanga, Kilwa and Dar es Salaam and the destroyer squadron there is at sea to protect the capital."

Wenig raised an eyebrow. "And us?"

We are to patrol Lake Victoria to protect Mwansa and destroy this new ship if possible. We are also to be prepared to reinforce L-102 on the coast if necessary."

Wenig nodded but Max broke in, "And what about Togoland Herr Kapitan? Is there to be no reinforcement?"

The captain turned to him. "I'm afraid not. We had only token forces there and we've lost contact with those already. High Command always knew it would be impossible to protect Togoland. Any reinforcements now would be wasted. It's too bad; Togoland is quite valuable for the Fatherland. It exported significant quantities of food."

Wenig spoke up. "So what's our next move with this new ship, sir?"

"They're working around the clock on *Gazelle* but it's going to be some time before she's ready for battle. *Antelope* is patrolling off Mwansa. The two of them together will stand a better chance against this new ship. Until then we'll do what we can. We've beaten up her base. That will make it harder for her to refuel and resupply. I think it's time we tried a night attack. Perhaps we can catch the enemy at anchor off Kisumu."

Max smiled and Wenig nodded. The captain nodded as well. "That's all gentlemen we launch at 1700. You may see to your duties." The two Leutnants saluted and left the office.

Ten hours later Max was pulling on a heavy leather coat over his uniform. It actually felt comfortable to put it on. It was cool here inside the hull at altitude. There was a steady draft as air moved through the girders and around the giant gas cells. His coat on, he turned and an enlisted man handed him a leather helmet.

The captain entered. He edged around the large metal shape in the center of the compartment and came up to Max. He had to shout to be heard over the roar of wind coming from the partially open hatch below the compartment, "Are you ready Max?"

"Yes, sir. I'm quite comfortable working from the "cloud car.""

The captain nodded. "I know you're familiar with navigating from it but this time you may be under fire. If things get too hot, let us know and we'll pull you up."

"I'll be fine, sir." Max put on his helmet and saluted, and the captain returned it. Max then climbed up the ladder placed on the side of the car.

It was a strange vehicle. Five meters long, it was teardrop-shaped and made totally from light-weight aluminum. The elongated tail tapered to a point and had four small fins to stabilize it. The observer sat in an open cockpit protected by a small glass shield protecting him from the wind stream. These 'cloud cars' were built specifically for navigators to be lowered below the airship so that they could see below cloud layers and navigate on dark nights or in inclement weather. Max had worked with them operationally over the North Sea. He smiled as he remembered their nickname

Once strapped in, Max gave a hand signal to the crewman standing by. He waved in return and the roar of the wind increased suddenly as the lower hatch was fully opened. Max pressed the button on the handset and waited.

After a pause he heard a tinny voice reply, "Captain here."

Max spoke loudly, "Cloud car ready deploy, sir."

"Very well. We're going to lower you five hundred meters to begin with."

Max acknowledged and waited. Seconds later he felt a jerk as the car descended through the floor hatch. Once it cleared the underside, Max felt the pull of the wind. The car was connected to the cable by three mounts on the topside of the car, two forward and one aft of the seated observer. They met at the cable overhead. A telephone line was also attached to the main cable. In addition to being very windy under the airship, it was dark. Looking up Max could see the belly of the giant ship receding away from him. Alone in the dark it could be frightening, but Max had done this before and stayed calm. He picked up his binoculars and began scanning ahead and down to the dark lake. They were over the bay leading to Kisumu, patrolling northwest at 2,000 meters and perhaps 50 kph

The stabilizing fins did their job. They kept the car from spinning and pointed forward. Max had been in cars buffeted by crosswinds and it wasn't pleasant. Tonight, there wasn't much wind and the car was quite steady. A half-moon wouldn't rise until later. For now, the sky was very dark. This would help conceal the Zeppelin from below but it also made visibility on the dark water poor. As Max scanned ahead he listened for the ship above him but heard nothing above the whistle of the wind.

They flew northwest with Max checking in every fifteen minutes. After an hour Max spotted lights on the horizon directly ahead. It must be the lights of Kisumu. Apparently, no one was worried about night bombing attacks. He called it in and was acknowledged. As they neared the port Max spotted a few small boats anchored in the harbor; probably fishing boats. Visibility was good over the harbor from the lights of the city. There was no sign of the mysterious warship.

As they cleared the city and moved over the dark African veldt the phone buzzed.

It was the captain. "The enemy ship isn't there. We are going to reverse course down the bay, if we don't spot her we will patrol out over the main lake."

Max acknowledged and the ship slowly turned southwest. As they swept over the town, it appeared they were unnoticed. All was quiet. Once again over water, Max scanned ahead with his binoculars. There were scattered clouds forming close to their altitude. Max called the control car and asked to be reeled out to the limit of the cable. This was quickly accomplished and soon he was hanging a full 800 meters below the Zeppelin. He looked up and could barely make out the airship above him in the darkness and scattered wisps of cloud. At that altitude with the wind-stream it was cold, but he was comfortable in his long coat.

An hour later they were nearing the entrance to the bay and Max had still sighted nothing. He was growing stiff in the cramped cockpit and he attempted to stretch. Nearly dropping his binoculars over the side; he didn't try that again. He was picking up the handset to report nothing once again when a flash of light somewhere below drew his attention. He lifted the glasses and scanned the dark water. He was beginning to think it had been his imagination when he saw a brief flash to port. He reached for the phone and called for a fifteen degree turn to port and a reduction in the engines to idle. Soon he felt his forward motion slowing. He continued to scan the area where he had seen the flash.

Max was startled when the flash came again, right in the center of his field of view. He recognized it instantly. It was actually a burst of sparks from a ship's funnel; a ship that was running totally dark. He reached for the phone.

"Captain here."

"Sir, we have a large ship running totally blacked out 10 degrees to port, range approximately two kilometers."

"Understood, can we attack?"

"Yes, sir. But I can't guarantee a hit. We'll be coming in across its starboard quarter. I suggest a series of continuous salvoes. I also recommend an altitude of 1.600 meters."

There was a pause. "Very well. We'll drop three bombs every two seconds on your command."

"Understood, stand by." Max kept his glasses fixed on the darkness where he had seen the funnel sparks. He looked in vain for a wake from the propellers. He saw nothing so he had to assume the ship was throttled back to very low speed, perhaps only a few knots. As they closed he began to make out the dim shape of the ship, a darker shadow on the dark water. He called in a small course change and gave the ship a one-minute standby. In his head he computed bomb fall time as forty seconds. If they could walk a string of bombs diagonally across the ship's path, they had a chance.

Max could hear nothing but the wind singing past the car. Hopefully the British could hear nothing either. The handset gripped in his hand, Max called in, "Stand by for drop." He was acknowledged. He gripped the handset hard. They had missed in two attacks. They mustn't miss now.

The shadow was very close now. He could make out more of the ship. His car was going to pass just ahead of its bow at 1,600 hundred meters. As he started to speak, Max clearly heard an alarm bell from the ship below. They had been seen. Max yelled into the handset, "Drop! Drop now!" He could hear the captain repeating his order and then there was silence. Max knew the bombs were dropping past him in the darkness but could see nothing. Instead, he leaned over the side to watch the shadowy ship.

Multiple lines of tracers suddenly reached out from the ship probing upwards. There were a half dozen and Max was sure they were all converging directly on him. Then the first bombs arrived. Three large explosions threw up tall water spouts. In the flash from the bombs, the enemy ship was lit up for a split second. The bombs were short. Seconds later the next three bombs arrived. More explosions; closer to the ship. Yellow tracers flashed just above his head and Max bit down on his lower lip. Now there were larger flashes in measured sequence as their two pounder guns opened up. Max was transfixed as the third salvo of bombs landed this time very close to the ship's starboard side. The towers of water actually cascaded down on the deck.

Seconds later, the fourth salvo of three bombs landed, this time just past the ship. There was another fountain of water and then a bright flash from somewhere on the bow. A hit!

Max pressed the button and yelled into the handset when it was picked up, "A hit! We hit her!"

There was tremendous noise from the explosions and flak bursting around him and he missed whatever the reply was.

In a moment the voice on the other end came again. "Repeat. Repeat your last transmission!"

Max calmed himself, "I repeat we have a hit on the ship's bow. We are past the ship. Cease bombing."

He twisted around and saw another group of bombs fall past the ship. He felt the car's speed increase. They were also turning gently to port. Max refocused his glasses on the enemy ship. It was easier this time. There was a small fire burning on her bow. There were also still many tracers arcing up from her toward the Zeppelin.

The intercom buzzed. It was the captain. He wanted directions to bring the ship under them for another attack.

Max told him, "If we have the ordnance I think that dropping across her as we just did will work again. Dropping a long series like that will likely get us more hits, sir."

The captain's voice came back calmly. "We dropped eighteen 50 kilograms on the last run. We have plenty left."

Max acknowledged and began planning the next run. The ship was moving more swiftly now. It was hard to judge in the dark but he had to assume at least twelve or more knots. They would have to drop earlier this time. Following his directions, the airship made a large circle and came around toward the enemy's starboard side. The Zeppelin was also cruising faster now as she straightened up for her run. Max had a firm target now. But it appeared that the fire on the forward deck was getting smaller. Their crew must be getting it under control.

They were two kilometers off when a searchlight on the ship snapped on. Tracers started to close in on the car again. Max gave the Zeppelin a standby order. Tracers zipped past and he felt something clang into the car behind him. He was speaking almost continuously into the handset calling out distance and course changes. Finally he said, "Twenty seconds to drop." He was acknowledged. He counted under his breath and spoke into the phone, "Drop! Drop n—"

Suddenly there was a flash and a bang. The phone was torn from his hand as a red-hot knife slashed his arm. His face smashed into something hard. Max was dazed and felt as if he was falling. Slowly he oriented himself. The car swayed back and forth and was being buffeted up and down. It was tilted over at a strange angle. His arm was throbbing and his vision was blurred. He looked up and could blurrily see the belly of the airship. It loomed above him. Then he realized it was so large because it was only a hundred meters off. He was being reeled in.

Max was worried about his arm and terrified about his vision but he twisted around with his good hand to find the handset. As he did, he realized that the reason the car was leaning over to one side was that one of the three tethers holding it to the main cable had parted. Max gulped as he finally found what was left of the handset. It had been cut in half by a bullet or piece of shrapnel. Moments later he was finally reeled into the lower compartment. It was quiet and seemed very bright in the ship.

He tried to smile as Leutnant Wenig appeared beside him speaking softly, "It's all right Max. We've got you."

Things got a little hazy after that. He was helped out of the car by gentle hands and led to the dressing station where an enlisted man trained in first aid dressed his arm. Eventually the captain arrived. He listened to the rating's report. Apparently, the same piece of shrapnel that had cut the handset in half had slashed through his arm and wrist. He had bandaged it up but Max would need to see the surgeon on their return. Max looked at the captain, "What happened, sir?"

The captain shook his head. "The intercom went dead. I dropped another series of salvoes. We didn't see any more hits and we couldn't contact you so I ordered the car up."

Max sat up. He was a little dizzy and his arm was starting to throb again. "But what about the attack? Are we going back in?"

The captain shook his head. "Over half our bombs are gone. With the cloud car out of action we can't get low enough to do any damage. Did you see any hits from the second attack?"

Max shook his head. "I'm sorry, sir. The car was hit just as you dropped. I didn't see anything after that. We got a solid hit on the first run. It started a fire on the foredeck."

The captain nodded. He looked Max over carefully. "It must have been pretty rough down there." Before Max could think how to answer that, the captain said, "Get some rest. We'll be back in Tabora in a few hours." He nodded and left the compartment.

The next day Max inspected the damaged cloud car in the hangar at the Tabora airfield. He decided it looked a lot like he felt. His arm was in a sling but was feeling better. The surgeon had said the nasty slash along his wrist and hand would heal but leave an ugly scar. The worst danger was from infection in the warm climate. His face was still sore and bruised from smashing into the wind screen. Looking over the cloud car he shook his head. There were several bullet holes through the aluminum hull. There was also a larger hole in the left side where something had torn through the hull, hit the handset and cut one of the cables, nearly taking off Max's hand in the process.

Leutnant Wenig walked into the hangar. He had just overseen the removal of the cloud car and walked up to Max shaking his head. "She took a beating. You're lucky Max."

Max nodded and patted the side of the battered little car. "I know. When I was dangling there below the ship all I could think of was the other cables snapping and me dropping straight down in the dark, just like a bomb." He smiled weakly, "Back in training we called these things 'flying bombs.' It doesn't seem very funny now."

Wenig smiled. "They are kind of shaped like bombs with those stabilizing fins. I wonder how much explosive you could stuff in one of these." He and Max exchanged grins.

"It's a good thing we had a spare car here at the base. Is it all hooked up?"

Wenig nodded. "Yes. The captain's taking us up for a patrol of the lake this afternoon. We'll test the new car then."

"I wish I was going along."

"The Doctor says you'll be back on duty in a few days." Wenig clapped Max on the shoulder. "Don't worry Max, we'll save some of the enemy for you. Hurry back."

When he had left, Max sat down on a crate of machine gun ammunition and stared at the damaged cloud car. Something about the conversation was bothering him. He thought for a moment and suddenly sat up straight. Could that work? It was insane but it just might be possible. Max left the hangar in a hurry.

At sunset Max watched the L-107 land and moor at the tall mast. It was winched down and the crew disembarked. He needed to speak to the captain about his plan but decided to wait until later.

Now Max entered the captain's office cap in hand and a paper rolled up under one arm. He saluted. "I'd like to speak with you, sir."

The captain set down his pencil and closed his logbook. "All right, Max.

Have a seat. How are you feeling?"

"Fine sir. I'll be ready for duty in a couple of days."

"Good. What can I do for you? You're not worried about the other night are you? You shouldn't be. You did a good job."

Max flushed slightly. "Uh, thank you, sir. Actually, I have a plan to attack the enemy ship I thought you should see."

"The Phantom? We could use something; she's eluded us three times. I personally am getting tired of fooling with her."

"The Phantom, sir?"

"That's what the crew is starting to call her. That's another reason to be done with this ship. It's bad for morale when the enemy starts to take on an air of invincibility."

"Yes, sir. That's why I've thought of something new for our next meeting."

The captain looked interested. "What are you thinking of?"

"Well sir, we can't get hits from high altitude, and it's too dangerous to go in low. Even at night our chances aren't good. But I was thinking that if we could direct our bombs...or one big bomb it would increase our chances."

Captain Trautloff looked skeptical, "How could that be done?"

Max stood up and unrolled his paper. "I've made a drawing of what I have in mind, sir."

The captain stood up and leaned over the drawing and calculations. He studied them for a moment. "This is your plan? Do you realize how dangerous this would be?" Before Max could answer he continued, "Is this even possible?"

Max nodded. "I believe so, sir. The car is already being repaired. I spoke with maintenance today about building a model for testing. It will take some work but I believe it is a way to get a decisive hit against the enemy."

Trautloff looked sharply at Max. "And I suppose you will pilot this... thing?"

"Well, I am the most qualified, sir."

Trautloff looked thoughtful, "How long will it take?"

"Uh, several days, I would think, sir."

The captain then gestured to Max's bandaged hand. "And will you be ready?"

"Yes, sir. I'll be ready!"

The captain sat back down in his chair and turned to stare at the map of German East Afrika for a moment. Then he turned back and fixed Max with his eyes. "All right, go ahead with these modifications. I will then inspect it and make a decision. I promise nothing though."

Max saluted. "Yes sir. Thank you, sir. I'll get started right away." He left the office smiling.

The next week Max was busy. He spent long hours running between the hangar and the wood shop. Meanwhile the L-107 went out every day on patrol. Sometimes it was over the lake searching for the enemy. Other days it was patrolling the northern border looking for troop movements or possible incursions from the British. Each evening the captain and Leutnant Wenig came to check on progress. Wenig especially took a keen interest in the cloud car modifications. It finally dawned on Max that the captain expected Wenig to take charge of the car if Max wasn't ready to fly it. This worried Max; it was his idea and he was determined to see it through.

By the third day the model was finished and Max started his testing. The model cloud car was nearly a meter long and quite detailed. One of the mechanics was a wood worker in civilian life and had done a fine job on the model. It differed from the real thing in several aspects. The stabilizing tail fins were much larger. There were also two horizontal stabilizing fins forward near the nose. Max had it weighted down to his scale calculations.

That day as soon as the L-107 had lifted off Max started his tests. He climbed to the top of the mooring mast and attached a long horizontal arm. While mechanics piled hay in a large heap below, Max suspended the model from the arm by a long cord. The cord connected to the model in only one spot rather than three as on the real cloud car. The model slowly rotated from the cord into a slight breeze blowing across the airfield and pivoted into the wind just like a weather vane.

Max looked down and one of the naval enlisted men waved. He took a breath and pulled the end of another trigger cord. The model released and fell downward. It wobbled a bit and then stabilized pointing straight down and plummeted fifteen meters into the pile of hay. He was already climbing down as the sailors ran over to retrieve the model.

On the ground Max examined the model. It was undamaged save for a few scratches around the nose. Max immediately climbed the mast and repeated the test. Again, the model quickly stabilized and fell straight down. Max realized what would happen if the full-size car were moving through the air at 50 kph. It would fall nose down but in a huge arc, just like a bomb. Max shook his head 'flying bomb' indeed.

The model cloud car was nearly a meter long.

Max took a screw driver out of his pocket and removed the screws holding the forward stabilizers. He adjusted them into a new position and re-tightened the screws.

Once more he climbed the tower and hung the model. Max waved to his ground crew. He consulted a piece of paper and shouted down directions for them to move the hay pile. A few minutes later the pile of hay had been moved considerable distance to one side. Max jerked the cord and the model fell. This time the model did not plummet straight down, instead it angled off to one side headed toward the hay pile. Max smiled but was surprised as the model overshot the hay and smashed into the ground nose first. When Max saw the model, he knew testing was over for the day. He sent the model off to be repaired while he scribbled down figures in his notebook.

Three days later Max's calculations were complete and he was ready for the final test. He had learned a lot. The cloud car modifications were also complete and it was ready to be installed back in L-107. He had just climbed into the cockpit of the modified cloud car when the captain and Wenig entered the hangar. They stepped onto a platform next to the car.

Max looked up proudly. "We are ready, sir."

The captain looked the car over carefully. It had been painted a dark gray with a single word in white on each side of the nose. The larger tail fins were now moveable and there were rectangular stabilizers on each side of the nose. They were about fifty centimeters wide and a meter in length. He looked at Max and asked, "Will it work?"

"Yes, sir. I'm confident it will."

Wenig looked skeptical. "How will you steer it?"

Max pointed between his knees, "We have connected the moveable tail fins to this control stick." He moved the stick side to side. "This moves the vertical surfaces and this moves the horizontal surfaces." He moved the stick forward and back. The two officers craned their heads to watch the fins move. Max continued, "This will allow me to actually steer the car as it moves under the Airship. Very similar to the control wheels in our Zeppelins. Now I can make fine adjustments to my course or compensate for a last minute turn from the target." He smiled confidently. The captain rubbed his chin thoughtfully.

"What is the payload?"

"One hundred fifty kilograms, sir." The captain looked interested as Wenig reached out to touch one of the forward fins, "What are these?"

"When a bomb is released, it falls in a large curving arc, propelled by forward momentum and gravity. These fins provide lift to the nose of the cloud car. This flattens out the curving arc and allows the car to fall on a straight course. I can adjust them to flatten or steepen the angle of the descent." Max reached to a lever on the left side of the car, pulled it out of a notch in the mount and moved it forward to the next notch. The forward fins moved downward.

Wenig looked impressed. "What do you call them?"

"I call them winglets."

As Max climbed out of the car to stand beside the two officers the captain nodded. "You've done a fine job with this Max, we'll get it aboard this afternoon."

"That's fine Herr Kapitan. There is only one thing more. I need you to drop the model from fifty meters over the airfield while moving. I will measure where it lands. It will be the largest measurement I have and will give me additional accuracy for my drop angle."

The captain nodded then pointed at the nose of the car. "And what is this?"

Max looked slightly embarrassed, "Well, uh the men felt that uh...." Max colored slightly. "Well, the men felt it need a name, sir."

The captain nodded, "So...the *Wasp*." Max glanced at the word painted in white on the nose, *Wespe*.

"Yes, sir."

As the captain turned away, he smiled, "Well, let's hope you sting the enemy hard."

Wenig clapped him on the shoulder. "Dropping the car might just work Max. I just hope you don't go with it."

Max thought to himself, "I do too."

The next afternoon the L-107 was cruising over Lake Victoria at a thousand meters. Below, Max could see two ships; one ahead to port and one to starboard. *Gazelle* had been repaired: she and her sister ship *SMS Antelope* were now out scouting for the enemy ship. It was uncertain if the two ships together would be a match for the British ship but they were there only to scout. L-107 and its new weapon would lead the attack.

Max was nervous but tried to look as casual as the captain. The final test had gone well. Cruising over the airfield at 50 meters, the airship had released the weighted model over a set spot. On the ground Max had watched it fall free. It had wobbled for a moment then stabilized and planed away at a forty degree down angle. It fell as if on a tight rope and plowed into the ground. With the help of a sailor Max had measured the actual horizontal distance covered during the fall and added it to his notebook. It was the only large-scale test he would get. The model had been smashed to pieces. Max regretted that. It would have been nice to save it.

The crew was excited as they searched the lake. Crew members passed words of encouragement to Max. He should have been proud. Instead, he felt as if the weight of the world was bearing down on him. He grew tenser as the day wore on. He was secretly relieved when the captain decided to turn back for base at 0200. *Antelope* and *Gazelle* would remain on the lake searching while remaining in radio contact.

Back at base the crew refueled and replaced ballast before tumbling into their beds. Max slept fitfully for a few hours but was wide awake when there was a knock on his door at 1300 the next day. The first officer stuck his head though the door.

Wenig looked excited. "Let's go Max. *Antelope* has sighted the enemy. The captain wants to launch immediately."

Max jumped up and grabbed for his clothes.

Thirty minutes later L-107 launched and turned north for the Lake. At altitude, the captain briefed Max. "*Antelope* and *Gazelle* have confirmed identity of the enemy. They engaged briefly but are withdrawing south attempting to pull him closer. They are about here." He pointed to a spot on the chart. "About 190 kilometers north of Mwansa." Max nodded. They would be there in four hours.

Time passed quickly. The crew was at battle stations and there was an electric feeling throughout the ship. The two German warships gave steady radio reports. The enemy was still following them south; the three ships exchanging gunfire at extreme ranges. No hits had been made by either side. As they closed the range, the captain slowed the airship. He wanted to meet the enemy after dark. At sunset they were very close. Max estimated they were within thirty kilometers of their ships when they received a message from *Antelope*: The enemy had broken off pursuit and turned north.

The captain steered toward the bearing of the radio transmission and at the same time ordered the airship down to five hundred meters. As the brief tropical dusk deepened, they spotted the two German warships. The captain slowed to almost hover over one ship. Maintaining radio silence, he used a signal light to give his orders to the warships' Captains. Soon they were headed north again at 70 kph and an altitude of 2,000 meters, the two warships following behind.

The time had come. Max saluted and requested permission to man the cloud car. The captain returned the salute and nodded. Max climbed the ladder into the hull of the great airship. It was loud and breezy here as he made his way aft toward the winch room. Crewmen called out well wishes. Max hardly heard them. All he could think of was what an idiot he was for coming up with this crazy idea. He tried to look confident but wasn't sure he was fooling anyone as he entered the winch room.

Max nodded to the crew and examined the car and cable. The cable was attached to only one point just behind his seat. There were now two handles to the left of his seat. Pulling one would release the car and send it plummeting on its final journey. The wind screen had been removed for streamlining. He bent and looked at the nose. Several metal spikes studded it. These were the contact exploders. Max was careful not to touch them even though he knew that it would take an extremely hard blow to set off the explosives packed in the car. Satisfied, he placed a leather helmet onto his head and swung a leather harness over his shoulders and between his legs. Before getting into the cockpit he reached out to touch the freshly painted words on the nose. Perhaps it would bring him luck.

Once in the car he felt carefully around. It was a tight fit. The control stick was between his knees. At his insistence a compass and an altimeter had been installed. Packed under him and in front of his legs were approximately 150 kilograms of high explosive. If he hit anything it would make a heck of a bang, Max thought as he buckled his seat belt. He attached the heavy leather belt that dangled from the cable above his head to the back of his harness. It was somewhat uncomfortable but in the end it was the only thing that might save him.

Max glanced at his watch; it was just after 1900. He was about to test the telephone connection when he was surprised to see the captain enter the compartment. He walked directly over the car and leaned down. "Is everything ready here?"

Max nodded. The captain continued, "The moon is nearly full and will be rising soon. We're at 2,000 meters. The forecast is for scattered clouds at about 1,600 meters. That should give us cover. Below us you'll hopefully have good visibility. I'll try to go lower if I can. The rest is up to you."

Max nodded again. "I'll do my best, sir." He was surprised when the captain thrust out his right hand.

"I know you will. Good luck Max. I'll see you on the other side." Max shook the hand and wished the captain luck as well. He saluted Max and left.

Minutes later the captain was on the intercom ordering the car lowered. As soon as it hit the wind stream below the airship Max had to grab for the stick. Without fixed fins, the cloud car was unstable in the wake of the ship. Now Max had to control it manually. He had no experience with this and for a few minutes it was all he could do to keep the car from spinning out of control. He quickly learned to make small corrections with the stick. Gradually the car settled under his touch. He was surprised at the sensitivity but hoped it meant he would be able to make precise corrections…if he ever got the hang of it.

As he grew more experienced in handling the control stick he began searching the dark water below. He had a good view across the water, at least when the moon shone through the clouds. The sky was at about forty percent cloud cover. Looking up he could barely see the shadowy form of the Zeppelin through the clouds. He glanced down at his instruments and was surprised to find he couldn't read them in the dim light. It hadn't occurred to him to have them illuminated. Max bent forward; his nose almost pressed against the gauges. He was at 1,200 hundred meters and headed northwest. As he watched he felt the car being buffeted and the compass needle swung around. He compensated with the control stick. The captain was turning northeast as he zig-zagged in a search pattern.

Max checked in regularly with the ship. On his third check in the captain said he was lowering the altitude because the clouds were lower than they had thought. Max bent forward as the altimeter unwound to less than 1,000 meters. Nodding, he picked up the binoculars to scan ahead.

Suddenly, off to port, he could clearly see the enemy ship caught in the bright moon light as it sailed out from under clouds. Max grabbed for the handset and called in the sighting. Within seconds the car was buffeted as the airship turned toward the enemy. Max kept a firm hand on the control stick and kept the car headed directly at the enemy. The wind streaming past him fell off as the captain slowed the great ship.

Max continued calling in his corrections as they neared the target. Estimating the target's speed he called in for a reduction to 30 kilometers per hour. He wanted to come in directly behind the enemy slightly above their speed. He estimated the distance to their target at less than two kilometers when suddenly a beam of light stabbed out from the ship pointed into the sky. Someone on the ship must have heard the throttled back engines of the Zeppelin. The searchlight probed upwards past the cloud car. Max could see it reflecting off the thin clouds.

He was just congratulating himself on remaining undiscovered when the searchlight swept across the car. Max was momentarily blinded. The ship below him erupted with lines of tracers reaching up toward him. This was quickly followed by the fire from the two pounder guns. Squinting into the light, Max saw the range closing. He reached down to the winglet handle and moved it forward one notch just as the searchlight steadied on him. He threw up a hand to shield his eyes but immediately clamped it back on the control stick as the nose of the car began to rise.

Max cursed as he struggled to maintain level flight. The winglet was pushing the nose up and flak was bursting around him throwing the car from side to side. Pinned in the light, the streams of tracers were rapidly converging on the car. The nose wandered and he pulled it around to the right. The ship below him was closing fast; too fast. Max grabbed the handset and shouted into it, "Slow to 25, repeat slow to 25!"

Fighting to get the nose down, Max felt the car jerk; then again and again. Squinting against the glare he saw a hole magically appear in one of the winglets. They were getting the range! He jerked the stick back; the nose of the *Wespe* rose sharply. He counted to three, and jerked the stick back down. He desperately hoped that his movements might throw off the gunner's aim. He glanced over the side and realized he was about eight hundred meters behind the ship. In the glare of the searchlight it was now easy to read the altimeter: still just under a thousand meters. He reached over his head and jerked hard on the leather belt to make sure it was still connected. He then picked up the handset and called the airship and yelled, "One minute to drop!"

Dropping the handset, Max reached for the winglet knob to steepen his drop angle. As he touched it a line of tracers tore past the car, one bullet punching through the side and tearing into his forearm.

Max screamed and grabbed his left arm. The moment he let go of the stick the car began yawing and pitching about. He immediately grabbed for the stick while cradling his wounded arm against his chest.

Damn! He needed to drop in just seconds. His arm screamed in pain as he grabbed the winglet handle and jammed it one notch forward. Fighting for control against the buffeting he glanced over the side of the car. Six hundred meters. A line of tracers flashed past the nose. He needed to call the airship but he was getting light headed. He didn't have much time left. Instead, gritting his teeth against the pain he unbuckled his belt and grabbed hold of the release handle.

Max concentrated on the target. He could barely see it through the glare of the searchlight. Flak explosions were bouncing the car around and the release handle was slippery with blood. Max gritted his teeth against the pain and gave a silent prayer as he pulled the handle. The car jerked and dropped away, smacking him painfully in the knee as it fell. For a second he was spinning in the glare of the searchlight, and then it was suddenly quiet.

He was swaying back and forth below the airship in darkness. Suddenly he remembered the *Wasp*. He looked frantically down. The enemy was in bright moonlight. Max then sighted the cloud car as the light caught it. His heart sank; it was going to miss the ship. It was going down too steeply.

As he watched there was huge flash in the very stern of the ship. Three seconds later the loud bang of the blast reached his ears. Max's jaw dropped. It had worked. The *Wasp* had struck the enemy. He waved and yelled in triumph. His arm didn't hurt and he felt like laughing. He got control of himself as he realized the ship was growing smaller. Someone must have decided to reel him in. He squeezed his arm and looked up wondering if this was what a fish felt like as it was reeled toward the boat. This was his last thought before he passed out.

Max was unconscious as they brought him aboard. Crewmen swarmed around. He didn't see the L-107 swing around and deliver a bombing attack on the nearly stationary ship from seventeen hundred meters. She dropped twenty bombs in a salvo. At least three and perhaps four hit the ship. As the Zeppelin swung away, fires could be seen burning in the ship's superstructure. The captain nodded, the fires would give *Antelope* and *Gazelle* a good aiming point.

The next day Max was resting in the military hospital in Tabora. His arm was in a sling. It still hurt although the doctor had given him something for the pain. He was thinking about getting up when the captain came to the door. As Max struggled up, the captain waved him down. "I thought I'd drop by and see how you're doing Max."

Max tried to look confident. "I'm fine, sir. It was kind of you to come."

"Nonsense. I'd do it for any of my men. How is your arm?"

"Fine, sir. The doctor is going to let me out of here in a couple of days. He says it isn't broken and should heal just fine." Max smiled. "At least it was the same arm again."

The captain nodded. "Good, we can't have our navigator lolling about in the hospital. There's work to be done."

"Work? The ship isn't badly damaged is it?"

The captain waved his hand. "Nothing serious. A few holes in the cells from flak but no one hurt."

Max could not contain himself, "Sir if I may ask, what happened after I uh, passed out?"

The captain smiled. "We saw the flash from the explosion. Once everyone quit yelling and cheering someone finally remembered to pull you up. You had bled a lot but the first officer got you bandaged up while we made an attack on the ship."

Max leaned forward expectantly. The captain continued, "She was on fire in the stern and moving very slowly. She didn't even attempt to evade as we dropped on her. We hit her hard with at least three bombs." He looked thoughtful. "I believe your flying bomb must have disabled her rudder and perhaps damaged her propeller." He looked back at Max and said firmly, "You did fine work out there Max. You should be proud." He smiled. "The crew certainly is. Most of them are out celebrating now."

Max felt his face coloring at this praise, "But what happened to the enemy, sir?"

"Our ships were coming up fast as we left. We received a radio message from *Antelope* not long after. Once they opened fire, the British ran up the white flag. Our ships took off the crew and sank her by gunfire." The captain put on his cap and made for the door. Once there he looked back. "Get well, we need you. Intelligence is expecting more trouble from the British. There's more work to do." He nodded and left. Max lay back down and closed his eyes.

More work to do? He'd better get some sleep then.

PART TWO

STRIKING BACK

"Careful with that line!" Oberleutnant Max Von Clausen called out to the crew of sailors lowering the large crate to the ground. The wooden crate was the largest item in the supplies that had arrived on the supply Zeppelin from home. The huge airship had landed before dawn at the airfield at Tabora, home field of L-102 and Max's L-107 bringing fresh dispatches, mail, medicines, ammunition and other supplies. She had also brought replacement sailors and soldiers to reinforce the defense of Deutsche Ost Afrika, the Kaiser's most important overseas colony.

It would depart that afternoon with reports to the high command and military casualties bound for home. Max had met most of those casualties while he spent two days in the hospital. That was why it was so important to quickly complete unloading of the Zeppelin. Many of those men were sailors from *SMS Gazelle* that had been badly wounded in battle with a mysterious British ship on Lake Victoria. He absently rubbed his left arm. He had been wounded while helping sink that same raider on a dangerous night mission. The scars were fresh and it was still quite stiff but the base doctor had cleared him for duty. Now the trimly built, brown haired young officer was supervising the unloading of the last piece of cargo from the soon departing Zeppelin.

As the crate reached the ground the sailors leapt forward to release the securing cables. Max watched as the cables were reeled back into the airship then stepped up to the mysterious crate. "What is it Herr Leutnant?" Max frowned as he looked over the markings stenciled on the wooden sides. There was the insignia of the Imperial German Naval Air Service as well as several series of numbers. Glancing at the manifest in his hand Max said thoughtfully, "All it says here is 'auxiliary observation vehicle.'"

"Another cloud car, sir?"

Max shook his head and smiled, "Let's find out. Gruner! Hand me that pry bar."

"Jawohl, Herr Leutnant." Taking the pry bar from the sailor, Max inserted it into a seam in the crate and heaved. Nails screeched and the wooden slat moved. Max grimaced as pain ran up his still healing arm. One of the enlisted men immediately jumped forward to take the pry bar from him, "Let me, Herr Leutnant." Max released it and stepped back hiding a smile. Since the incident over Lake Victoria when he had been wounded while piloting the make shift flying bomb, the crew had been quite protective of their young hero. It gave him a good feeling to have been accepted so quickly into his new crew.

Ten minutes later the men were piling the last wooden slats into a pile. Two men carried forward a meter and half long wrapped object and laid it on the ground in front of Max. He quickly helped them pull away the canvas wrapping and cloth padding beneath to reveal...what? It was a flat, smooth rectangular object perhaps a 100mm thick. It was made of light weight plywood and was hollow; one square end had rounded corners. The other end was open with dangling metal cables hanging out of the

41

interior. The young leutnant frowned. It reminded him strongly of one of the small winglets he had helped design for the "Wasp" the one of a kind flying bomb used to sink the British ship less than a week before.

He turned and helped the men unwrap more of the crate's mysterious contents. As more parts were unwrapped Max was surprised to realize it was a glider. He had seen photographs and had actually seen one flying at a glider club the year before. The unpowered vehicles were mainly used by flying clubs and considered for recreation only. He had heard rumors that the Naval Air Service was doing experiments with them but he certainly hadn't expected an actual glider to wind up here.

"What is it, sir?"

"It's a glider," Max said wonderingly. There were confused looks among the men. Shaking himself into action, Max pointed at the large wrapped parts lying in front of him and waved an arm, "Let's get these over to the hangar. This is going to take some assembly."

He grabbed hold of one end of a large piece and helped another man carry it toward the nearby hangar. In minutes they had all the parts inside and Max was wondering where to start when Kapitanleutnant Peter Wenig stuck his head into the hangar and called out, "Better get over to the radio room, Max. Something's going on." He then disappeared. Ordering the men to continue unwrapping the glider parts Max hustled across the airfield toward the headquarters building. He scanned the sky but saw nothing. Were the British attacking? The air was still in the late morning and both L-107 and the supply Zep swung gently at their moorings. Nothing else stirred in the warm air.

Inside the HQ building Max found the hallway leading to the radio room crowded with both sailors and officers. He wormed his way through the crowd to a place near the radio room door where he could hear voices from within. Everyone in the hall was whispering. He turned to a petty officer and whispered, "What's going on?"

The tanned veteran whispered back, "Dar Es Salaam was attacked this morning. The reports are just coming in." Max felt his pulse quickening. Ever since hostilities against the British had commenced they all had been expecting a surface attack on the colony. Max was actually surprised it hadn't happened sooner. If it had he might have missed the action. At least he was now out of the hospital and could be a part of any upcoming missions.

The tall form of Korvetten Kapitan Trautloff, commander of L-107, appeared in the doorway and everyone fell back to give him room. He marched down the hallway and stopped at the outside door. Looking back he rapped out, "Wenig and Von Clausen, my office in a half hour!" He put on his cap and left the building. The crowd quickly broke up and Max fell into step with the first officer as they crossed to their quarters, "What's going on Peter?"

"Dar Es Salaam was attacked before dawn; naval bombardment by heavy guns. The British must have slipped past our cruisers in the dark. Our destroyer squadron sortied and there was a heck of a battle."

Max tried to sound calm as he asked, "Any damage reports?"

Wenig shrugged, "Reports are just coming in and are confused. There's talk that we lost a destroyer."

Max was speechless for a moment then continued, "What's the Kapitan got in mind?"

Wenig smiled, "He wants to hit back, of course." They had reached the officer's quarters and Wenig turned toward his room, "Better get cleaned up and change that uniform." Max looked down at his soiled tropical uniform and agreed.

A half hour later the two officers were in Trautloff's office and listening keenly. The captain had a handful of radio messages in his hand as he spoke, "The situation is this. Dar Es Salaam was bombarded by enemy ships this morning before dawn. Targets were commercial piers, the naval base and government buildings in the town. Casualties were heavy in the city and damage heavy in the port area. Our destroyers sortied and attacked what were identified as British cruisers. One of our destroyers was sunk; damage to others is still unclear."

He sorted through the radio reports and continued, "The East Afrika squadron closed at dawn and engaged the retreating enemy. We are just now receiving reports of damage." He put down the reports and looked at his officers "L-102 is searching for the retreating enemy now. We are to prepare our ship for immediate action. The admiral is considering our options and I expect orders momentarily. Max, familiarize yourself with all the charts from Dar Es Salaam north to Mombasa. Be ready for take-off in one hour. Questions?"

Wenig raised a hand, "What kind of bomb load, sir?"

"Full load. We won't be traveling far. Most likely we'll be scouting for our cruisers but we should be ready for targets of opportunity. Anything else?"

The two officers had none. They saluted and left Trautloff's office.

By 1500 hours the great airship was ready to launch. The gas cells were filled, ballast taken aboard and she carried a full load of bombs. Max was at his navigator's station across from the radio room in the control car under the Zeppelin's nose. He looked up as one of the new crewmen brushed by him toward the rear of the control car. He was carrying a long black gun in his arms. Max glanced aft and saw him installing the machine gun on its swivel mount at the rear of the car.

They had received six new crewmen in the last few days. Since they were now on a war footing the High Command had seen fit to augment the crew of L-107. Max had barely met the new crewmen. He would have to correct that. The captain believed his officers should know all the crew and be aware of their strengths and weaknesses. He turned back to his charts. Ready reports were coming in from all over the ship and only minutes later Kapitan Trautloff gave the command, "Schiff Hoch!"

The ground crew released their lines and the great airship slid smoothly into the sky pushed by its six powerful Maybach engines. As they climbed toward cruising altitude of 1000 meters the captain called out, "What's the course, Max?"

Max was ready with his answer, "095degrees, Herr Kapitan."

"Very well," Trautloff passed the order to the helmsmen and lifted his binoculars to look ahead. Their course to the coast plotted, Max took a few minutes to gaze out the port near his station. He never tired of looking out over the African veldt. The continent was so huge. There weren't the many cities and rivers he was used to seeing over Europe. Instead there were vast vistas of open country teeming with great herds of animals. Max shook his head; the peaceful scene did not reflect the sharp battles going on now between the Fatherland and Great Britain here in Africa. He turned back to his charts. It was nearly six hundred kilometers to the coast; about five hours flight time. He leaned back and tried to relax.

During the afternoon they received several radio reports. The captain read them all and passed all relevant information along to both Max and Wenig. It was just after 1800 hours and the sun was just setting directly behind them when a new message came in. Trautloff read it and moved to the intercom. Lifting the handset he summoned the first officer to the command car. Soon Wenig slid down the ladder into the car and looked at the captain. He nodded and led the way aft to the navigator's station. With both of his officers present the captain indicated the radio message in his hand, "We have just received a signal from headquarters in Tabora. Apparently one of the enemy cruisers was badly damaged in last night's action. Reports indicate that it was hit by a torpedo. Another cruiser was damaged by gunfire. L-102 has been shadowing the enemy force and they have separated. Two cruisers have been withdrawing north all day. L-102 is sticking with them. They are probably headed for Mombasa. The other two cruisers have been moving at slow speed and have entered the harbor at Zanzibar."

Max and Wenig exchanged glances at this news. The captain continued, "We have been ordered to attack any warships in Zanzibar harbor tonight. If they are damaged, they will be anchored, probably alongside piers. If so, they will be excellent targets. Max, I need a course for Zanzibar. Peter, slow us down. I want to attack near midnight when the enemy has settled down."

Wenig moved forward to give engine orders while Max grabbed for his dividers and a ruler. He quickly looked up, "115 should bring us in just to the south of the harbor, sir."

Trautloff nodded, "Good. That should be fine." He turned and went forward. Max let out a long breath. He suddenly had that sinking feeling. They were going into action again. Since Max was not only the navigator but the bombardier as well it would be his responsibility to direct the bombing. He stood up and moved toward the bombsight to check it over.

Shortly after 2330 hours the dark bulk of Zanzibar Island was sighted off the port bow. The L-107 was flying with two of her six engines at idle and the rest at one third power. They were at 1000 meters and on their present course would pass south of the islands harbor west to east. Max moved over to the port side of the car and found a port where he could use his binoculars. Wenig was there as well. Behind him the captain ordered the remaining engines to slow ahead.

It was a clear but moonless night as the great airship drifted slowly toward the island. Focusing his glasses Max quickly found the harbor. The land was darker than the water so he could see the rough outlines of the shallow bay. Scattered lights illuminated the city behind it. Although a blackout must certainly be in effect, getting the natives to follow it would easier said than done. Max knew the Germans had the same problem in their colonial cities on the mainland.

Most of the dozens of dim lights scattered through the town were likely fires or lanterns. Still, they gave enough light to give perspective to the harbor.

Max concentrated his vision where the dim lights abruptly ended on the assumption that that was where the sea meant the harbor docks. As he peered through the glasses he heard a low exclamation from the first Leutnant, "I've got it! A large darkened ship anchored against the sea wall."

A second later the captain spoke, "There is another large darkened ship anchored in the roadstead perhaps a half kilometer from shore." Chagrined he hadn't seen anything yet, Max scanned the harbor and finally saw the shadowy shape the captain had made out. He turned as the captain spoke, "We'll swing around and attack from the east. Max, call out when you have the target in your sight. Peter, I want a salvo of 100 kg bombs on Max's command."

The officers saluted. Max headed aft to the bomb sight while Wenig climbed into the hull where he would supervise the drop. The bombsight was a clumsy device set into the cabin floor just forward of the aft machine gun positioned near the rear of the car. Max uncovered it and began checking his settings.

Meanwhile the Zeppelin was turning in a wide circle over the island. Glancing out the port Max could see only the scattered lights of small settlements amid the foliage as they passed over the darkened island. When they had steadied again on course the captain appeared at his side, "I'm going to bring us in at 50 kph, Max. We'll be attacking from the east and pass out over the harbor. Max dialed in the indicated speed and queried, "Altitude, Herr Kapitan?"

"It doesn't look like we've been sighted. We'll go in low at 1500 meters." Max nodded as he adjusted his dials accordingly, "I'll be ready, sir."

Trautloff clapped him on the shoulder and with a nod went forward to stand behind the forward helmsman. It was dark in the compartment. The only sound was the quiet movement of the gunner behind him and the low-voiced commands coming from the front compartment. The captain was giving out course correction and engine commands that were quickly carried out. Max looked through his sight. He could see nothing below him but darkness. He wasn't worried though. The view through the sight was very narrow and he knew he wouldn't see anything until the last minute.

Forward the captain called out, "Standby! Approaching the port area in one minute."

Max's palms were wet but he didn't attempt to wipe them. Instead he kept his eye pressed to his sight. There! He started seeing scattered lights in his narrow view. They were passing over the town. He knew the lights

Max uncovered it and began checking his settings.

would disappear over the dark water. He was keying on this.

Suddenly in his other eye Max saw glaring light outside the port. A searchlight! They'd been spotted! The captain's calm voice called out "Steady." And a second later, "Twenty seconds! Standby!"

Max was fixed on the sight. The car bounced once, then again. He didn't move. He knew from experience that the jostling was flak rather than rough air. He licked his lips and concentrated. There! A band of pure darkness had entered his sight. He called out loudly, "Target in sight! Standby." He could hear the captain passing on orders to other parts of the ship.

A second later Max suddenly could make out a long straight shape in his sight. Below it were scattered lights, above it darkness. It had to be the enemy cruiser anchored against the shore. It moved into his crosshairs and he yelled, "Drop! Drop! Drop!"

The words were barely out of his mouth when a glaringly bright light stabbed out from the ship below. They had turned on a searchlight. Simultaneously lines of tracer began to reach up from the target. In the excitement Max hadn't heard the captain repeating his command over the intercom to Leutnant Wenig in charge of bomb release but he knew it must have been given. He scrambled to a nearby port. He knew from experience that he wouldn't be able to see the bombs land through the sight.

Bomb fall from their altitude was about twenty five seconds and Max barely made it to the port in time. As he craned his head downward he saw a flash followed by others. In the strobe light of the flashes he could see the enemy cruiser clearly. It had taken multiple direct hits. He resisted his instinctive urge to yell in triumph and concentrated on spotting the fall. He saw tall water spouts as some bombs overshot the target and exploded in the sea near the enemy. Max wasn't too worried about this. He knew that near misses sometimes did underwater damage to the target as well.

The command car lurched and Max looked around. He now realized that the car was filled with light. Looking down and to port he was blinded by glare. The ship anchored in the harbor must be the other enemy cruiser. It had them pinned in a searchlight. The captain yelled out, "Full power on all engines! Elevators to full up!"

Max grabbed for something to hold onto as the nose of the Zeppelin pitched up sharply but smoothly. He couldn't feel the increased vibration of the engines but he felt the increase in speed as they accelerated. He also felt several a jarring shudders through the ship. He frowned. That didn't feel right.

He had just turned to go forward when something tore through the floor of the car just missing his foot. There were shouts and wind was suddenly whistling through the car. Someone was screaming nearby. Shaking off shock Max leaped to the rear of the car. The gunner was down on the deck holding his leg and screaming. In the dim light Max couldn't tell how bad it was as on his hands and knees he pulled at the man's hands while he talked to him, "It's all right. Let me take a look." He pushed the man's hands away and felt slippery blood everywhere.

Max grimaced and pulled one of the man's hands back onto the leg, "Press here! Hard!" the moaning man did just that. During flight the crew wore loose beltless coveralls without pockets. The captain though, insisted on his officers wearing full uniform for morale purposes. Max was thankful for this as he fumbled under his long coat for his belt. Finally getting hold of the leather he whipped it off and quickly wrapped it around the wounded man's thigh. He pulled it tight while the man groaned in pain, "Sorry. It's got to be tight."

Until that moment he had been working only by the glare of searchlights entering the cabin. Suddenly a beam of light appeared over his shoulder focused on the wounded sailor, "We're here Herr Leutnant! Let me take a look." Max allowed himself to be pushed aside as the ship's medical rating bent over the wounded man. As he stood up he could see that a machine gun slug must have passed through the man's inner thigh. It must have nicked an artery from the amount of blood all over the man's coveralls.

Seeing that the medical rating had things under control Max made his way forward. He felt a little queasy but took a deep breath to get himself under control. He realized the interior of the car was darker now. They must have flown out of the reach of the enemy searchlight. The captain was talking on the intercom. He finished and hung up the handset. In the control room light Max saw the surprised look on his face, "Are you all right Max?"

Max nodded, "Ja, Herr Kapitan." Max looked down at his hands. They were covered in dark blood. He couldn't tell what his dark blue uniform coat looked like but he was sure there was blood on it too. He attempted a weak smile, "I'm fine, sir. It was the gunner who was hit."

The captain glanced aft and nodded. He turned and looked forward, "We're headed north. I'm going to swing around and make another run on the harbor. We'll come in from the north, give the docked cruiser a few more bombs and attack the anchored ship. Is the bomb sight operational?"

Max replied, "I think so, sir. I'll go and check." The captain nodded and turned to pick up the handset as the intercom buzzed, "Captain here… Yes?" A pause, "Do the best you can Peter and keep me informed."

Max headed aft but quickly pressed himself to one side of the corridor as two crewmen helped the wounded gunner past. His leg was bandaged and he seemed only semi-conscious but at least he was alive. The medical rating gave Max a quick nod as they went past. Reaching the bomb sight Max pulled a flashlight off its wall mount and examined the important instrument. A quick check seemed positive. It had been a near thing though. Wind whistled through a hole in the floor centimeters from its base.

Relieved that the delicate instrument was all right Max found his binoculars and looked out the starboard port. They were north of the harbor turning in a great circle. The harbor was easily visible due to fires set by their first attack. Buildings were burning along the waterfront piers. Focusing the glasses Max could see the enemy cruiser was hard hit. It was burning fiercely amidships and there was a smaller fire burning aft. There was a lot of activity in the water around it. Several small boats and lots of what Max was sure were people in the water. He wanted to cheer but suddenly felt nothing but sadness. Those men in the water were no longer the enemy they were now just survivors. He lowered his glasses unable to look any longer.

He looked up and saw the captain making his way aft. He moved to his sight and setting down his binoculars he tried to look impassive. The captain glanced out the port and then looked at Max, "They're alerted now. We're going to have to go in higher this time. Set your altitude at two thousand meters and your speed at 65 kph."

"Max nodded, "Very good, sir." He hesitated, "Uh, sir. The first cruiser is done for and…and there are men in the water." He felt his face flush. The captain was now going to tear his head off for questioning orders but he had to speak up.

The captain's face had gone very still and Max braced himself for a tongue lashing. Instead Trautloff spoke quietly, "I know Max. Forget the first cruiser. We're going in on the second cruiser only. We have to disable them before they slip anchor and get away."

He turned away quickly and Max was glad the captain couldn't see the relieved look on his face. He quickly entered the new information into the bomb sight and sighted through it. Everything checked out fine. Meanwhile he could hear the captain giving maneuvering orders. Picking up his binoculars again Max looked forward. He could plainly see by the light of the burning ship the second cruiser anchored a several hundred meters offshore. It was not moving but he could see smoke above the ship amidships. Since she had not been attacked the smoke must be from her funnel. Within minutes she would be underway.

The ship was certainly alert. Searching tracers floated upward into the darkness and not one but two searchlights probed the sky. It was still very dark and hopefully with all the firing they couldn't hear the Zeppelin's approach from the north.

Setting the binoculars down Max moved back to his sight. A minute later the captain called out, "We're closing on the target. Stand by Max!"

Max pressed his eye to the sight and waited. Visibility across the water was better this time and he was sure they would hit the enemy hard. The ship appeared at the top of his sight and he sang out, "Enemy in sight! Stand by!"

The ship was buffeted and he could see flashes outside of the cabin with his off eye. Max concentrated. The ship was creeping close to the center of the sight. He called out, "One minute to drop!"

There was a bang and the whole control car jumped. The ship was close and Max hung onto the sight, "Thirty seconds!"

Max held his breath. The ship was almost in his cross hairs. Then the enemy's aspect began to change. They were moving! Max yelled out, "Drop! Drop now!" He scrambled to his feet and was thrown against the side of the car as the ship was shook by an explosion near it. He got to a viewport in time to see the enemy cruiser sail out from the center of several water spouts. She shook off the cascading water and began to move faster. She was lit brightly from the searchlights and flashes of her guns firing in every direction. Max could even see the huge white battle ensign flying from her foremast. They had hit her though. Max could see a fire burning aft of her single funnel. Her speed was increasing quickly and Max swore softly to himself.

Moving forward he reached the captain just as he was hanging up the intercom, "Max we're losing gas out of several cells. Get up top and give Wenig a hand." Surprised Max "jawohled" and headed for the ladder leading into the hull. Inside it was loud and windy as always. Crewmen were running to and fro. He grabbed one and yelling to make himself heard asked for the first Leutnant. The crew men yelled back, "He's up between cells ten and eleven." Max let him go and worked his way aft. He reached the dark space between the huge gas cells. Within the huge ring framework was a network of reinforcing wires and ladders going upwards.

Max climbed a ladder and within minutes found Wenig. He worked close to him and yelled, "What can I do?"

Wenig gave a final order to a crewman who went crawling upwards and turned to Max, "Go aft between eleven and twelve and see if they have the leaks under control!"

Max ducked his head and yelled back, "Right!"

Reversing course down the ladder he moved along the catwalk to the next set of gas cells and climbed upwards. He found several crewmen crawling around the huge metal ring using flashlights to scan the huge gas cells. They would stop and listen; if they heard the hiss of a leak they would locate it and slap a patch on it. Max pitched in and for the next half hour was as busy as he could remember crawling through the darkened space searching for leaks and helping the repair crew.

Finally they had plugged every leak they could find. A tired Wenig met Max on the main catwalk and they moved forward. They dropped down into the control car and saluted the captain. Wenig then spoke, "All leaks plugged, sir. They're temporary but they'll hold until we can get home. Cell twelve lost a lot of gas. Ten and eleven not as much but they lost a good bit as well. I think we can hold altitude but we're not going to be climbing much higher."

Trautloff nodded, "Good work you two. Pass that on to the men as well."

Max spoke up tiredly, "What about the enemy, sir?"

"They're headed north-northeast. Speed at 20 knots. We're shadowing from behind. We can't seem to climb much above 1600 meters. The enemy is still on fire aft so we can track them easily but I think they're getting that under control."

Max thought to himself, "Damn! I thought we hit them hard enough to slow them down." He spoke aloud, "Now that we're repaired are we going to attack again?"

Trautloff turned to his first officer, "How many bombs are left."

Wenig wiped his hand tiredly across his face, "We only have twenty-four 50 kgs left, sir."

Trautloff was thoughtful for a moment, "She's still got a lot of speed and we don't have surprise anymore." He shook his head, "I think we've done all we can. Let's head for home. Peter, what about the wounded?"

"Two men, sir. One caught some shrapnel and that gunner that Max helped save. Dietrich says they're both going to be okay, although they'll need hospital time."

"Very well. Max, give us a course for home." He raised his voice, "All engines to full! Left full rudder!" Max turned tiredly for his navigation table.

On his way to the hangar, Max paused to look at the airship. L-107 swung gently at her mooring. Men were clustered underneath her sorting through equipment. Other men supported by ropes were suspended on her sides repairing and painting patches on the airship's hull. He watched the activity for a moment before continuing on to the hangar. Once inside its cool interior he sighed and looked over the mass of parts scattered across the hangar floor. Picking up a set of blue prints and an instruction book he set to work. The airship had made it home late yesterday afternoon. After over twenty four hours in the air the captain had given the crew the night to recover as repair crews swarmed over the Zeppelin. This morning the crew had joined them.

Max had been told to survey the new glider and brief the captain with a plan concerning its assembly and use. His first act was to survey all the parts, the assembly drawings and the operational manual that had been shipped with it. By lunch he had inventoried the parts and had a rough idea what it would take to get the glider assembled. Surprisingly it was bigger than he had thought. It also had the capacity to transport two men in tandem seats. It had a single mid-mounted wing with quite a long wingspan. It had a simple low mounted tail and two partially enclosed cockpits. Altogether quite impressive Max thought. But impressive for what? He had no idea what they were going to do with it.

After a quick lunch Max was back at work. He studied the operations manual and realized quite quickly that the flight controls were similar to the simple ones he had designed when building the *Wasp* flying bomb. The actual flight characteristics were unknown but the operation of the controls had to be similar.

By dinner time he had a plan. He gathered up his paperwork and headed toward the captain's office. His knock was quickly answered and he entered and saluted. Trautloff put down his pencil and waved Max to a chair. When he was seated the captain asked, "Well, have you got our new toy put together yet?"

Max didn't know how to reply for an instant, but then realized his commander was having some fun at his expense. He smiled and said, "If you're in hurry for a ride I am sure something can be arranged Herr

Kapitan." Trautloff laughed briefly and shook his head, "Tell me what we have and why they've sent it to us."

Max quickly related what he had accomplished that day finishing with, "I have no idea why the glider was sent here, sir. But if I can have a couple of riggers from the crew I can probably have it assembled in two or three days. The question is what does the High Command want done with it?"

Trautloff looked thoughtful for a moment then picked up a piece of paper and looked at it, "Perhaps our new officer could tell us…if he was here."

"New officer, sir?"

A glance at the paper, "Yes, it seems we have been assigned one Leutnant Ernst Brandel who was to accompany the glider and be assigned to our ship. Unfortunately he seems to have been misplaced somewhere along the line."

Max did not know what to say for a moment, "You mean he's missing, sir?"

"I mean he was not aboard the supply Zeppelin when it launched from Germany."

Max said thoughtfully, "I would assume he was trained to fly the glider."

"Yes, he also must have specific orders for us regarding it. I have sent a radiogram to High Command inquiring about the Leutnant's whereabouts. In the mean time I want you to work on assembling it and readying it for flight." He looked thoughtfully at Max for a moment before continuing, "If something has happened to our new Leutnant, can you fly that thing?"

Max was surprised and took his time answering, "Uh, well sir, I have seen civilian gliders flying and from the look of the controls I believe the theory of control is similar to what we used for the *Wasp* but actually flying it? That might be difficult without experienced…uh, advice." Max hated looking doubtful in front of the captain but his brief experience in piloting the *Wasp* had been both terrifying and exhilarating. He didn't know how he felt about repeating the experience.

Trautloff looked thoughtful, "Take two men and continue the assembly of the glider. We won't worry about flying it until we find out what's happened to our new officer." He looked at his watch, "Come, it's time for dinner." He stood up and reached for his cap on the coat tree. As they left the office the captain said, "We'll stop by the hospital on the way. I want to check on the wounded." Max readily agreed as they headed across the airfield.

For the next two days Max and two of the Zeppelin's aircraft fitters worked hard assembling the glider. They had lots of impromptu help as many of the Airship's crew stopped by to see the new "toy" as someone nicknamed it. Other officers from around the field also found excuses to come by the hangar. Often Max would draft the visitors into helping out by lifting up one of the awkwardly long wings or moving the fuselage about the hangar. This seemed to discourage visitors somewhat.

The first thing they assembled was the fuselage so Max could begin studying the piloting area. Most of the simple instruments Max was familiar with. There was an altimeter, a speed indicator and of course a compass. There were two gauges though that he had never seen before. One was a larger than normal and had what seemed to be a small replica of glider seen end on; wings to each side and a small tail. Another was a vertical gauge with a horizontal red line crossing it and notations at bottom and top reading "Down" and "Up." He made a note to look through the accompanying paperwork for references to these.

The most interesting things were the controls. There were pedals on the floor connected by cables to the tail rudder. Max had installed these himself and he knew that they moved the rudder from side to side. When "Flying" the *Wasp* he had used the "control stick" for this. There was a small control wheel just below the instrument panel that rotated left and right. Cables ran from it to control surfaces on the wings, which they had just attached. This Max assumed would do just what the simple "control stick" he had designed for the Wasp.

The glider was approximately 6 meters long with a wingspan of over 12 meters. The wings and control surfaces were made of fabric covered wood. While the fuselage was made of aluminum tubing covered by fabric. A recessed single wheel protruded from the belly of the fuselage. The glider could be flown by one man but there were controls in front of each seat. It was light weight for its size and could easily be maneuvered around the hangar by the three men. Max still couldn't figure exactly why it was here though. It was too big to fit into the Zeppelin's cargo areas even if the bomb racks were removed. If it was here for testing, they were certainly going to need a pilot. He shook his head and hoped that the High Command knew what they were doing.

It was late in the afternoon and they were threading control cables through the second wing when Wenig strolled in. Repairs on the Zeppelin had gone on round the clock and she had been pronounced ready for flight the night before. He stood there looking thoughtfully at the glider. Finally he said, "I wonder how much explosive it will hold?" Max leaned his head out from under the wing where he was tightening a control cable and looked up at the officer, "What do you mean?"

"Well, if we're going to dangle you underneath the Zeppelin in this thing we need to know how much explosive to put in it." Max looked sourly at the first officer, "Very funny Peter. I don't think the High Command sent this thing down here to be a flying bomb. Besides I doubt if they've even seen our combat reports on the *Wasp* yet."

Wenig rocked back and forth on his feet and grinned, "Still it's a lot bigger than the last flying bomb. I'll bet you could sink a cruiser with this one. They'd probably give you a Knight's Cross for that."

Max gave his harasser a dirty look and ducked back under the wing, His sour voice came from there, "Don't you have some brass to polish or some bullets to count?"

"I'm afraid not. The ship's all ready to fly. By the way, that's why I came by. We're flying tonight. The captain wants us in his office for a briefing in an hour." Max jerked upward and banged his head on the wing. He swore and leaning out glared at Wenig, "Why didn't you say so? I've got to get cleaned up." He crawled from under the wing mumbling and dusting himself off. Wenig stepped back and shook his head, "You could use a good bath."

Max grimaced as he turned to his two assistants, "You two go get cleaned up. It looks like we're flying tonight." The crewmen dropped their tools and headed out of the hangar grinning at the two officers as they passed.

Forty-five minutes later the two officers were entering base headquarters. As they neared the captain's office they could hear a raised voice through the thin walls. Max whispered, "The new leutnant?"

Wenig nodded. Their missing Leutnant zur See had turned up on the supply Zeppelin earlier that day. Max hadn't met him but Wenig had. Outside the door Max leaned close and heard the captain's voice speaking in a commanding tone, "... and for your information Leutnant, the Kaiser is not running a passenger service here. It was your responsibility to ..." Max leaned back and grimacing at Wenig shook his head. Wenig shrugged and waved him on. The two continued on to the officer's lounge where they poured themselves cups of coffee and sat down in comfortable chairs. Max sipped his coffee and queried, "So where has our new man been the last four days?"

Wenig smiled, "It seems he missed the Zeppelin at Friedrichshafen. Something about getting lost on the train trip from Bremerhaven."

Max whistled softly, "The captain is not going to be pleased about that."

Wenig grinned back, "No, He's not."

The two chuckled for a moment before Max spoke, "So what are we supposed to do with him?"

Wenig shrugged, "Maybe it has something to do with the new toy."

Max nodded thoughtfully, "Maybe." Wenig then added, "What I want to know is, can he do anything useful? Is he even trained on Airships?"

A good question Max thought to himself. Further ruminations were interrupted by a loud voice from down the hall, "Wenig! Von Clausen! Are you out there?"

Max and Wenig jumped to their feet and hurried to the captain's office. Inside the captain was just seating himself. A rather short, red-faced officer was standing at rigid attention in front of the captain's desk. As the other two officers fell into place beside him Kapitan Trautloff looked up from some papers he was reading. To Max's eye he did not look happy, "Stand at ease, gentlemen."

The three officers relaxed slightly as the captain continued, "Max, this is Leutnant Brandel. Leutnant, this is Oberleutnant Von Clausen he will be your immediate supervisor." Max was surprised by this statement but remained impassive as the captain continued, "Leutnant Brandel has been assigned to us to perform testing of the new glider in conjunction with our ship. That however is for the future. Tonight we have a mission."

Max held back his excitement. Wenig spoke up though, "Where are we off to tonight Herr Kapitan?"

Trautloff stood up and moved to the large map of Africa on one wall. He pointed to a spot east of Lake Victoria, "We have been tasked to destroy the large radio mast at Nairobi. Our cruisers damaged the smaller mast at Mombasa when they bombarded it three days ago. The admiral wants to cut communications between London and their colony. We leave at dusk. Max get out your charts and plot a course. Peter is the ship ready for flight?"

"Fully ready, Herr Kapitan."

Trautloff nodded, "Leutnant Brandel you will have no duties on tonight's flight except to stay close to Max and learn what you can. You have been trained in Airships but have no combat experience at all, is that correct?"

"Uh, yes sir," answered the new Leutnant.

The captain looked at him sternly, "We'll remedy that situation tonight. This is a combat tested crew, Leutnant. Keep your eyes open, and you will learn a lot."

He nodded, "Schiff Hoch at 1750 hours. That's all gentlemen." The three officers saluted and left the captain who was already resuming his paperwork as they exited the office.

Out in the hallway Max held out his hand to the young officer, "My name's Max."

He took the hand and shook it, "I'm Ernst." As they shook, Max sized him up. He was slimly built and shorter than Max. He was also a few years younger by Max's judgment. Max indicated Wenig and said, "You've already met our intrepid First Officer, I take it?"

Brandel nodded as Max grinned, "A rough start, eh? Don't worry about it we don't all bite like the captain." Wenig nodded and said, "I've got to round up the crew, Max. See that our young adventurer doesn't get lost on the way to the ship." He turned and left chuckling audibly.

Brandel had gone red faced again. Max took his arm and led him toward the door, "Let's get you some gear." As they walked across to the supply building Max said, "The captain expects his officers to wear full uniform while flying instead of coveralls. You will need some felt boots though." He slipped Brandel a sideways glance, "How many hours do you have in Zeps?"

The young officer hesitated a moment before answering, "Other than training? Uh, about a hundred hours. I only graduated from Airship school a few months ago." Max winced internally but kept his voice light as he opened the door and ushered the young officer into the supply building, "Well, You're certainly going to get a lot of experience quickly here."

The airship had lifted off as the sun was setting. Max had put them on a course of 050 degrees northeast toward British East Africa. Young Brandel had stuck to him like glue as Max plotted their course. He asked a few questions but seemed to follow Max's calculations easily enough. Max took the time to brief him on local conditions and give him a few tips on getting along with the captain and the crew. The newcomer had asked him rather tentatively about the actions they had been involved in. Max told him a little about the last couple of week's actions but without too much detail. He would learn soon enough how crazy things could get in combat.

Their first navigational check point was Lake Eyasi just over two hours into the flight. Max checked it off the map as Brandel leaned over his shoulder. Then Max gave orders for a course for their next check point

Lake Natron. He pointed out features on the map and instructed Brandel, "Out here in the bush there are no cities and few towns. Rivers are also rare. Often lakes are the best navigational markers available. Navigation can be a challenge sometimes, especially at night."

Brandel nodded, "I can see that. Will most of our missions be at night?"

Max shrugged, "Depends on the mission. Bombings, yes. Long range reconnaissance will see a lot of daylight flying. Fortunately the British have no airships assigned to this part of Africa. I am surprised they haven't sent any yet."

Brandel looked curiously at Max, "I heard that you sank a British cruiser a few days ago." Max smiled, "We were lucky. She was damaged and we caught her at anchor. That's the good part about having air superiority. It's giving us an advantage now. But who knows what will happen next week." Max might have been mistaken in the dim light but the young leutnant looked a little paler to him.

Nearly two hours later the forward lookout relayed sighting a body of water ahead. Max moved to his chart and pointed their position to his student, "Lake Natron." He glanced at his watch, "On time." As he lowered his arm the captain loomed up beside the two officers, "How does it look Max?"

Max replied, "Nairobi is approximately two hundred kilometers away. Course 030, sir."

"Good. I want to approach from the east. Intelligence shows the radio mast is west of the town. We'll use the city as a final check point." Max nodded, "Very good, sir." The captain nodded and returned to the front of the car. Once he the captain had turned away Brandel whispered to Max, "He's pretty tough, isn't he?" Max swallowed a grin and said seriously, "The captain's a good man. Other than the ship he the only thing he cares about is the men. Do your job properly and you'll be all right." The young officer nodded thoughtfully.

Lake Natron straddled the border between the two colonies and as they passed over it the change in tension could be felt in the control car. They were over enemy territory now. Max stood next to Brandel and the two watched the dark veldt pass under them a thousand meters below. "It's so big," whispered Brandel.

Max agreed, "It's a lot bigger than Europe. You should see it during the day. It seems to go on forever." Brandel just nodded. In the control room forward the intercom buzzed. The captain answered and spoke briefly. A moment later the called out, "Max come forward and take a look at this." Max motioned Brandel to follow him as he went forward in the car. The captain was at the large starboard view port looking southeast through his binoculars. As Max came up beside him he asked, "What do you make of that, Max?"

Looking out Max could see what appeared to be a string of lights across the veldt. He lifted his binoculars and scanned until he found the lights in his view. The light came into focus and he spoke up, "It looks like a convoy of vehicles, lots of vehicles." He lowered his binoculars and stepped to the compass mounted on the wall, "Headed southeast, toward the border."

The captain asked, "Trucks, you think?"

Max once again focused on the distant lights, "Yes, sir. There are no roads out here to speak of. That many vehicles have to be military and they're headed toward the DOA." (Deutshe Ost Afrika) (German East Africa) He thought a minute and added, "That's the north end of the Bura hills. Kilimanjaro's out that way."

The captain looked thoughtful, "We can't break wireless silence now. After our mission we'll come back this way and alert our forces. With enough warning they can move an Askari regiment into position. Maybe two." He nodded to the two officers before turning away, "Thank you gentlemen."

As they resumed their positions over the navigator's table Brandel whispered to Max, "Wow, he's awfully calm." Max replied, "Like ice. When things get crazy it's something to remember." Brandel said nothing as Max bent over the map.

A half hour later it was time to make their final turn westward toward Nairobi. Max passed along the new course and the great airship turned westward. The captain ordered an increase in altitude to 2000 meters and told Max that would be their bombing height. Max motioned to Brandel and they moved aft to the bombsight. Once there he set the altitude and asked, "You're qualified in bombing right?" Brandel nodded. "Well, it's a little different out here. The trick is to stay focused. No matter what happens you keep your eye on the target. We can get thrown around quite a bit if we're taking fire. So stay focused, got it?" Brandel swallowed and nodded again.

Soon the captain called the ship to battle stations. It wasn't long until the lights of Nairobi came into view. Nairobi was the capital and largest town in British East Africa and Max had expected that there would be at least some lights to give a bombing reference but he was surprised at the amount of lighted buildings below them. If they were having a blackout here nobody had told the populace. With the town lit up, it was easy to find their way across the city. Max knelt by the sight with Brandel at his side. They could hear the captain conning the ship calmly. Soon he called back, "The mast is in sight. Two minutes!"

Max turned to say something but suddenly the cabin was lit up with bright light as they were caught squarely in the glare of a searchlight beam. Brandel looked both surprised and frightened. Max gave him a confident smile and bent over the sight. A moment later the control car was shaken by a nearby explosion. Max could see the flash in his free eye. Apparently the British had heavy flak guns in Nairobi. That was a surprise! He stayed calm and waited, the city unrolling beneath him.

The captain called out, "Target in sight. Two kilometers!" Max adjusted the focus. The car whole car jerked to one side from and explosion. There! He could see the wireless mast in his sight, quickly illuminated by the flash of gunfire. The British must have emplaced several guns in the vicinity of the mast. He called out, "One minute! Stand by!"

There was a cacophony of noise around and inside the car. The intercom was buzzing and flak was bursting around the ship. They were almost over the target and Max could see the mast creeping toward the center of his sight. A pause, then he yelled out, "Drop! Drop! Drop!"

He looked up. Brandel was hanging on to the side of the car while he stared out the port. Max lunged up and grabbed his shoulder just as the salvo of bombs hit. The multiple explosions lit up the hill occupied by the wireless mast and transmitting station. As he pulled Brandel away from the port another explosion rocked the control car shattering several of the glass ports. Neither Leutnant saw the giant metal mast sway and crash to the ground.

Within minutes the Zeppelin had moved out of range of the searchlights and was once again in darkness. The two young officers moved forward. The captain was taking a damage report. When he hung up the intercom he turned to them, "That was good work, Max. Now I need you to plot a course for the estimated position of that British convoy." He tuned to the younger officer, "Brandel, some of our communications are out. Take a flashlight and go forward to the nose and alert the observers to watch for the enemy column. When you've done that, report to Leutnant Wenig and see what you can do for damage control."

Brandel saluted, "Yes, sir," and made for the ladder. As Max turned away, the captain leaned in the radio room doorway, "Take this message to Headquarters Tabora: Enemy column sighted 70 kilometers southeast of Nairobi ..."

…he was surprised at the amount of lighted buildings…

An hour later things had settled down and the captain called an officers' conference in the control car. He started by asking for a damage report. Wenig reeled off the list of damages and summed up with, "We've patched all the holes in the cells but we've lost a good bit of gas. It's going to be hard to climb if we need to. There is also a lot of minor damage from shrapnel that will have to wait until we are back at base. We still don't have communications in many parts of the hull. We still have nearly fifty 50 kg bombs and we're ready for combat, sir."

"Good work, Peter. Pass my compliments along to your men. Max how far are we from that column?"

"We're nearing their last known position now, sir. I've projected a search pattern following that course. I imagine we'll come up on them within the hour. I'm afraid there are scattered clouds forming up at about 1500 meters. It may be hard to spot the column if they've laagered in for the night."

The captain looked at Wenig, "Is the cloud car operational?"

"Yes, sir. I just checked it and it worked fine."

"Good." The captain turned to Brandel, "Normally it would be your job to man the car Leutnant, but I think we need someone with more experience tonight." Brandel looked relieved as the captain turned to Max, "Max?"

"Yes sir, I understand."

"Good, man the car. Leutnant Brandel, you will man the bomb sight. To your stations, gentlemen."

Max followed the first officer up the ladder into the hull. Soon he was wearing his long leather coat and goggles and lowering himself into the replacement cloud car. As he cinched his seat belt tight he found himself missing the wooden control stick he had used when flying the *Wasp* on her one and only mission. He signaled Wenig who waved back and gave the signal to lower Max into the black night.

When the wind stream hit it the little car spun and bucked for a few moments before stabilizing in airstream below the airship. Looking up Max watched the huge ship recede away from him. The captain was flying the Zeppelin at 2000 hundred meters altitude. Far enough away to save it from small arms damage but more importantly as high as she would fly on the gas in the cells. When the cable was let out its full 800 meters Max picked up his binoculars and began scanning the dark ground ahead.

He checked in with the control car every ten minutes with a negative report. A half hour of fighting the wind stream and his cramped position later he was about to call in a third time when he saw a flash to his left. Swinging his binoculars around he saw what looked like a dim light moving slowly along the ground. Focusing he made out the shape of a man carrying what was probably a flashlight. Max scanned around that point and quickly located several large dark shadows amid the scrub bushes and trees. He grabbed for the intercom set. He heard a buzz and when someone picked up the other end he shouted, "Control, this is cloud car. I have blacked out troops at 090 to our course. Distance five to six hundred meters."

He was twisted around to keep his targets in sight as the Zeppelin passed to the west of the enemy headed southeast. The captain's calm voice came back quickly, "What is the enemy's strength?"

Max was counting as he replied, "Five, six, seven uh, I have at least seven large trucks parked and roughly camouflaged. There are probably more but I cannot identify them now. They are behind us now."

"Keep the enemy in sight. We're turning in one minute."

Max kept his binoculars trained where he thought the concealed enemy was. He felt himself swinging outward and knew that somewhere above the great Zeppelin was coming around in a wide circle. The captain had the engines throttled back and he could barely hear anything from above. Minutes later they were on a reverse course closing on the enemy's position. Max leaned forward the handset in one hand pressed to his ear and the other holding the binoculars to his eyes. The target was ill-defined and no doubt spread out over a large area. He concentrated until his eyes watered hoping for a sight. There! Another dim light moving away from a dark shadow. They were nearly on top of the British. He called into the handset, "Stand by, we're coming up on the enemy" Moments later the captain spoke calmly in his ear, "We have the target in sight."

Swaying beneath the Zeppelin in the little aluminum car was often exhilarating and sometimes frightening but it did give Max the best view of their target. Leaning over the side he couldn't see the bombs falling from the ship but he certainly saw them hit the ground. There was a series of flashes and he saw a bomb fling a truck into the air. Another exploded in flames from the direct hit of a 50 kg. bomb. Other trucks were burning and in the glare of the explosions and fires Max could see men running in all directions. Just that quickly the chaos passed under and behind them.

A buzzing caught his ear. The intercom was buzzing and Max rather guiltily wondered how long that had been going on as he lifted the handset to his ear, "Cloud Car."

"How did that look Max?"

"Very good, sir. I saw at least five trucks hit. Troops were scattering. The enemy was pretty dispersed though."

"Very well. We're heading for home and are reeling you up. Good work"

Max acknowledged and felt relieved. It would be good to be safely back aboard and headed for home. He felt the car jerk and could tell it was being reeled in. Seconds later the car jarred to a stop. Puzzled, Max looked upward but could see only the dark shadow still far above him. He waited impatiently for a few moments for someone to notice they had accidentally hit the stop button before he finally reached for the handset. It buzzed as his hand touched it. He answered, "Cloud car."

Leutnant, I'm afraid we have a problem." Max's heart beat more quickly but he kept his voice calm, "What is it, sir?"

"The winch has jammed. Leutnant Wenig thinks one of the damaged electrical cables has shorted out. He is attempting to locate the problem now. Stand by."

There was nothing else to do Max thought as he replied, "Yes sir."

Minutes passed as the Zeppelin and its dangling hatchling droned through the night. It was late and despite his leather coat Max was growing cold. There was nothing to do but wait so he tried to occupy his time by looking down at the terrain. Too bad it was night he speculated; the view in daylight would have been spectacular.

The captain called every few minutes to check on him but the longer he waited the glummer Max got. He had just about resigned himself to riding the five hours home dangling in the car when the intercom buzzed, "Cloud car."

"Leutnant, I'm afraid there's bad news."

Max gritted his teeth and squeezed the handset tightly, "What is it, sir?"

They can't track down the electrical fault. Wenig says the line was probably partially cut by shrapnel somewhere and then shorted out. They're still looking but it doesn't look good."

Max took a deep breath and said confidently, "That's all right sir. I can ride it out here until we get home. Then there will be lots of ground crew to assist me."

There was pause that chilled him, "Max, we cannot climb any higher and there is higher ground ahead." Another pause, "Do you understand?"

He did. The Bura Hills ran southeast of Kilimanjaro. To the north and west were other hills and higher ground.

"I understand sir. Can we turn north and take a longer way home nearer the lakes?"

"We can but we're still slowly losing gas. We've dropped nearly all our ballast. Sooner or later you're going to be dangerously low."

Max's heart sank, "What do you think, sir."

"The ship is not in great danger but you are. Before we can reach home you're going to be so low that you will be in danger from every tree and small hill in our path." He paused, "The first officer and I have discussed it and we have a plan. It's not one we like but we believe it gives you the best chance of survival."

Max swallowed, "Whatever is best for the ship, sir."

"Fine. We want you to guide us in as low as you can. We will slow to minimum speed...walking speed. When you are barely skimming the ground at our slowest speed, give us the command and we will cut the cable. The impact should be minimal." Trautloff paused, "It's risky Max but we feel it's the best option."

Max let out a sigh, "I understand, sir. I will be fine. I know you won't be able to circle back and pick me up." A pause, "Can you tell me how far off our forces are?"

"We're not sure. Colonial Command has dispatched two Askari regiments to this area. They could be only hours away but we haven't established contact with them."

Max took a deep breath and spoke firmly, "All right. Start losing altitude. I'll give you constant reports."

"Starting descent now."

Max let go his binoculars and leaned over the side of the car. It was getting lighter. The moon was rising in the east and visibility was fair. With the handset to his ear he gave continual updates to the Zeppelin as it gradually lost altitude. Soon he was skimming along only 20 meters over the ground. It was fairly flat here, the terrain broken only by scrub brush and trees. Mostly small trees but occasionally a towering acacia tree would loom suddenly out of the darkness. Ahead Max could see the ground rising to a range of hills. Here was as good as any place if he was going to hope for a safe landing.

They were traveling slowly but now he ordered the airship to drop speed to minimum. Soon the car had slowed to walking speed. Although skimming along less than 2 meters off the ground gave the impression of a much greater speed to Max who had ducked low in the tiny cockpit to avoid getting slapped by passing bushes. With ground rising he knew the time was close. He called up to the airship, "Control, stand by for cable release."

The captain's reassuring voice came back immediately, "We're ready Max. Good luck. We'll pass on your location to friendly forces. Keep heading south. You should run into them later today."

"Yes, sir. One minute." The ground was rising. It was less than a meter below the car. Suddenly the car plowed through a low bush and spun around before steadying. Max realized he wasn't going to get any lower. He yelled through the intercom, "Idle your engines!" He waited another thirty seconds as he felt his speed bleed off then yelled again, "Cut the cable!"

The intercom went dead as the car suddenly dropped. Max tried to get his hands up to brace himself but the car dropped suddenly, hit the ground and bounced a meter into the air. It came down again plowed through a large bush, hit a small rise and skidded to a halt 5 meters from a huge acacia tree. Max had been thrown forward sharply and smacked his face hard into the windscreen. He was slightly dazed and sat up just in time to get slapped across the shoulders by the falling cable. This threw his head forward and he again banged his head against the windscreen. He sat there stunned for a moment. It was dark and very quiet. There was dust rising all around him and he coughed as he unbuckled his seat belt.

Standing up rather shakily Max stepped out of the car holding his face. He shook his head; he was going to have another beautiful black eye, he just knew it. He stepped away from the car and looked around. The moon was rising in the east but the light it provided wouldn't last long. He couldn't see the Zeppelin in the dark sky and could barely heat its fading engines. He looked at his watch and saw that it was nearly four o'clock. In two hours it would be light. He took off his leather flight helmet and threw it into the car and unbuttoned his coat. He wouldn't need either on the trek south. By nine in the morning the sun would be blistering.

With his long coat off Max stretched and oriented himself by the stars. He took a long breath and started walking south.

The light was fairly good and Max had made good time at first. He knew that he had to cover as much ground as possible while it was cool and he set a good pace. The sun came up soon after six and he could see the country ahead. He had crossed a line of low hills and was in flat ground again. He walked on. He saw plenty of wildlife but no humans. He saw a herd of antelope and in the distance a family of giraffes. The animals saw him coming from a distance though so he never got close. By ten o'clock Max was suffering. His mouth was dust dry and he desperately wanted a drink of water. He finally picked up a pebble and put it in his mouth. He had heard from some of the old African hands that it helped keep your mouth moistened. It might have been true but Max couldn't tell. Soon he knew he couldn't continue in the heat. He swerved aside from his course and took shelter in the shade of a huge acacia tree. It didn't help his thirst but he felt much better out of the sun. His back against the tree the exhausted officer soon fell asleep.

When he awoke the sun was setting. He remained under the tree resting and waiting for it to cool. Finally he trudged off southward once more. Even in the cooler temperature Max was suffering. There were water holes and small lakes about and he knew had to find one soon. Soon after midnight he slumped down in exhaustion under a small tree. He intended to rest for just a few minutes but quickly fell asleep once again.

Max awoke to sun in his eyes. It was just rising above the horizon in a brilliant orange display. He struggled to his feet, his tongue thick in his mouth, when he was startled by a large flock of birds rising suddenly from a patch of green a hundred meters to the northeast. It took a moment for his blurry brain to connect the bright foliage with water but when he did, he half ran half staggered toward it. He pushed through the tall grass and fell into a moderate sized pond. Startled an antelope across from him sprang away in fright. Max plunged his head into the water and drank deeply.

Sometime later he got to his feet. It was amazing how quickly the water had restored him. He wasn't totally recovered but his brain was functioning again. He looked around and took stock. He had no idea where he was except that he had traveled twenty or more kilometers south and west of where he had been dropped. He was surprised that he hadn't come across any troops. At the moment he even would have been happy to meet up with British troops.

He was in a quandary. His recent experience had taught him that without water he couldn't go far. He had no way to carry water so he couldn't leave the water hole but how long could he survive here? As he watched he saw a small plume of dust to the northeast. He shaded his eyes with his hand against the sun and finally made out a vehicle heading his way. He immediately dropped to one knee. He looked frantically around for a place to hide but there was nothing but the waist high grass surrounding the water hole and a few scraggly trees. No cover at all.

Max crawled to where he could see through the grass. The vehicle was much closer now. It appeared to be an armored car. From the turret above the vehicle a man was looking at him through a pair of binoculars. Max knew he had been seen. As the vehicle neared he reluctantly stood up.

The car stopped about twenty meters off. It was a boxy four wheeled vehicle. Above and behind the armored driver's compartment was a round open topped turret. From the side of the turret protruded the barrel of a machine gun. There was a metallic clank and from around the back of the vehicle came a man in tropical uniform. He wore a pith helmet and carried a revolver. Max sighed and raised his hands.

Max sat in the hot vehicle on a narrow fold down seat with his hands tied. He was behind and to the left of the driver. Above him dangled the legs of the sergeant who commanded the Morris armored car that had captured him. Across from him sat a young private who leaned back with his eyes closed. Periodically he opened them to stare at Max before going back to his dozing.

The crew had not been unkind to him. He had been searched and questioned. None of the soldiers spoke German and Max's English was only fair. He pretended he spoke none at all and after a few minutes the sergeant had quit questioning him in frustration. While this was happening the other two soldiers had refilled their water sacks and canteens at the water hole. Within a half hour they were all in the car and headed northeast.

From the questions asked and the conversations among themselves Max had gathered the men were scouting for a British column, probably the one L 107 had attacked two nights before. The sergeant had recognized Max's uniform and one of the questions he had repeatedly asked was what had happened to the Zeppelin. Max had just shrugged and pretended not to understand. After a half hour of traveling, Max was feeling very low. He was a captive. Technically Germany and Great Britain were not at war. They had not been at war for over twenty years but that hadn't stopped either country from fighting these endless brush fire wars and skirmishes. Prisoners had often been taken. Sometimes they were quickly returned, sometimes they were traded for enemy prisoners and sometimes they were held in political limbo…sometimes for years. "So much for a promising career," he thought.

Max was snapped out of his reverie by the car slowing. The engine raced but the car continued to slow until it stopped. The driver continued to race the engine but they did not move. Finally the sergeant yelled down to him to cut the engine. In the silence he climbed out of the turret. A moment later he opened the armored door at the back of the car and yelled, "Everyone out!" The soldier motioned Max out and they both jumped down to the ground. He was momentarily blinded by the bright sun after the relative dark of the car and he shielded his eyes with his tied hands.

The driver and sergeant were standing by the car's back wheels arguing loudly. As he watched the driver kicked the wheel he was standing by and cursed, "Bugger!" Apparently, they had hit a patch of loose sandy soil and the car's back wheels were mired in the sand. The driver was complaining about not having four-wheel drive ability. Max pretended not understand this. Instead he watched the soldier watching him looking for any inattention. Unfortunately the young private's rifle remained casually pointed at Max the whole time.

Finally, the sergeant started giving orders. The driver untied two shovels that were tied onto the front fenders. Meanwhile the sergeant cut Max's bindings, much to his surprise. He was enlightened when the driver handed him one of the shovels and motioned him to follow. Soon Max found himself digging sand from around one of the armored cars rear wheels. The soldier with the rifle kept a close eye on him; unfortunately from well out of shovel range.

When they had dug long sloping channels in front of the wheels, the driver gave the shovel to his sergeant and climbed into the vehicle. Max stepped back and leaned on his shovel. The driver started the engine while the sergeant stood near the open rear door and yelled, "All right then. Give her a little gas!" The engine revved and the rear wheels spun. Then they grabbed and the car rocked forward. Sand flew up from the spinning wheels and the car fell back. The sergeant got a face full of sand and stumbled back cursing. The soldier near him laughed and got a dirty look in return. Max held his own smile and tried to look bored.

The sergeant yelled, "All right! That's enough!" The driver dropped the engine back to idle. The sergeant motioned Max forward, "Get in there and dig some more Fritz!" Max got down on one knee and shoveled sand from in front of the wheel. The sergeant did the same on the other side. When the trenches under the car were sloped enough the sergeant motioned Max back. He then yelled into the car, "All right then, we'll give it another go. This time put some pedal into it!" The driver revved the engine in response.

The sergeant took three steps back this time and yelled, "Go!" The engine growled louder and the car jerked forward. The wheels spun and Max thought it would fall back for a moment then it lurched up and out of the sand. As the car jumped forward the solider near him yelled in triumph. Max spun and hit him with the flat of the shovel in the chest. Caught totally off guard, the soldier took the blow unawares and was thrown onto his back. Max caught a glimpse of the sergeant's shocked face as he threw the shovel at him. The sergeant ducked as Max darted for the car. It had slowed to a stop twenty feet away. Max jumped in the car and pulled the rear door shut as a shot rang off it.

Inside the car the driver looked back in surprise and scrambled up out of his seat. He was off balance when Max caught him with a right to the jaw. He dodged a clumsy return blow and shoved the driver against the car's wall as hard as he could. His head hit the wall and he staggered. Max followed up with two punches that knocked him unconscious.

As Max climbed into the driver's seat, he became aware of someone banging on the back of the car and yelling. He shoved the car into gear and peering through the driver's visor he pressed the accelerator to the floor. The wheels spun and the car bucked forward. Steering wildly to throw off anyone trying to climb on the car, Max sped away. He didn't see the sergeant being dragged for ten meters while hanging on to the rear door handle before letting go to fall on his face in the dirt.

A minute later Max brought the car to a halt. A quick check showed him the soldier still unconscious on the floor of the armored car. Quickly he scrambled up into the open topped turret. The empty veldt stretched all around. The only thing he could see moving were two small shapes several hundred yards behind the car. Max thought for a moment as he rested his hand on the heavy machine gun. He had the car, capturing the crew as well seemed a bit ambitious as well as...greedy. Still, he couldn't leave them stranded out here without water. He had just gone through that and wouldn't wish it on anyone, even his enemies.

Dropping into the interior, he unlatched the rear door and swung it open. He then dragged the unconscious solider to the door and jumped down. Muscling the soldier onto this shoulder he carried him several meters and laid him in the meager shade of a large bush. Climbing back into the car, he located three canvas water bags and carried them over to the soldier. He found two pith helmets and tossed them out as well.

Wiping his sweating brow Max reached into the car and drank deeply from one of two additional canteens he found within. As he corked it he heard the crack of a rifle and instantly the clang and ping of a ricochet off the car's armor. He instinctively ducked. Looking over his shoulder he realized the two, probably very angry soldiers had run forward and were now only about three hundred meters away. That was close enough. Max dove into the car and dogged the door closed behind him. Starting the car, he shoved it into gear and drove off. He gradually swung the car around in a large circle and five minutes later he pulled up. Finding a pair of binoculars he climbed into the turret for a look around.

He quickly found the enemy soldiers and focused on them. They had revived their unconscious friend and had him on his feet. They had also found the helmets and water bags. As he watched Max could see them arguing among themselves and gesturing angrily. Some of the gestures were quite rude and directed in his direction. Suppressing a grin, Max scanned the horizon with the glasses. To the northeast he could see what appeared to be dust on the horizon; enemy troops? Very possible. To the southwest there was nothing.

Quickly he climbed back behind the steering wheel. The was a compass mounted in front of him and he turned the car until it was pointed south southwest and pressed down the accelerator. German forces had to be out here somewhere. He just had to find them.

An hour later Max climbed out of the car and glared at the rear right wheel. It was bogged down nearly to the axle in a patch of sand. He shook his head angrily. The view from the narrow, armored visor was limited and he had not realized he was running into loose soil until the drive wheels started spinning. Walking around to the left side he could see that wheel was on fairly firm ground. He wiped a tired hand across his eyes. He could probably dig the car clear if he had a shovel. Unfortunately, the shovels had been left behind with his former captors. Muttering to himself he climbed back into the car and searched for anything that might help. He found lots of tools; wrenches, a hammer, a jack, an axe, a pry bar but no shovels. He took a drink from a canteen and cursed under his breath.

Max shook his head. It seemed like the Gods of War had decided to torment him endlessly. Shaking his head, he grabbed the binoculars and climbed onto the top of the car. Standing atop it he slowly scanned the horizon. There was nothing ahead of him but rolling veldt; the same to the west and north. As he slowly panned to the northeast, a small cloud of dust appeared in his field of view. Freezing, he focused and waited. The sweat ran down his face as he stood there. Soon shapes swam into view. One, two, three, four...a lot of trucks coming his way.

Climbing down Max sat down in the shade of the car his back against a wheel and thought about the situation. Although he had more water than before, a canteen and a half, he had no hope at all of outrunning the motorized forces approaching. Likewise his hopes of hiding from them were slim. The country was too open. It looked like he had no options. Standing up he dusted off the seat of his pants and stared at the fast approaching dust. Damn! He slapped the metal side of the armored car with his palm.

He quickly jerked his stinging hand back and shook it. The metal was hard and hot from standing in the sun. Standing there shaking his stinging palm it suddenly occurred to Max that he did have an option.

Climbing into the car Max quickly scrambled into the turret. The gun was a Vickers. It's heavy barrel shrouded in a large cylindrical water jacket. A hose ran from the jacket into a square can of water mounted under the gun. A canvas belt holding shiny brass cartridges gleamed in the glare. Max yanked back on the charging handle mounted on the side of the heavy gun. A round flew upwards and clanged off the roof of the car. He nodded; the gun seemed very much like the old Maxim guns he had trained with. L-107 was armed with the newer air cooled MG34s and MG 15s but he could still handle something like this. He looked outward, the dust was closer and Max could see darker shapes in front of it. Dropping down he rummaged around the car until he found a pair of leather gloves. He also found several more belts of ammo for the gun. Closing and locking the car's door, Max climbed back behind the Vickers gun and draped an extra belt across his shoulders.

Now that the decision had been made, Max felt more relaxed. He couldn't hold them off forever. He might not even last long if they had artillery or heavy weapons but he would hold them up for a while. He had no idea where the German troops were but they had to be out there somewhere. If he could hold the British up here for even an hour it might let his own people get into position.

The British were closer now. He could make out individual trucks with his eyes squinted against the glare. They must have seen the car because they were coming directly toward him. Picking up the binoculars he could see the trucks clearly as they began to spread out. He had hoped they would close straight in on him; that way he could surprise them. Deploying meant they knew the car had been captured. So his three friends had been picked up. Max was glad for them. At least they wouldn't wander in the bush until they ran out of water.

He glanced at his watch. It was nearly noon. He could see the enemy clearly now. The range was less than a thousand meters. Within reach of the gun but it would be so inaccurate he would just be wasting ammunition. Better to wait. Something had changed though. Max picked up the binoculars and focused on the distant enemy. The trucks had stopped. Through the glasses he could see enemy infantry spilling out them and deploying. It wouldn't be long now.

Max waited. His shirt was wet with sweat and he wished sorely for sun glasses. He squinted into the glare. He could see the infantry clearly now. They were within five hundred yards. They knew their business Max noted. They were spread out and moving in short rushes. As he gripped the spade grips of the gun Max wondered idly if the airship had made it back safely? He smiled sourly; at least they had his replacement. Ernst was green but he would learn.

Max opened fire when the closest troops were four hundred meters out. As soon as he started shooting everyone went to ground. He fired in short bursts, as he had been trained, at any movement he saw. Rifle fire started coming in against him. He heard the crack of the rounds going over his head or the clang as they hit the armored of side of the car. He knew that the armor wasn't that thick but it should stop rifle or pistol fire. He would be all right as long as they didn't have anti-tank rifles with them.

He continued snapping off short bursts as the enemy closed in. He estimated there were over a hundred of them scattered across a couple of hundred meters. The last of the cartridges ran through the Vickers and it clicked on empty. Max fumbled with the unfamiliar catch before finally managing to get the feed cover open. He pulled the cartridge belt over his head and fed one end of the belt into the gun. As he slapped the cover closed and yanked back the bolt to chamber a fresh round, he could see men up and running, taking advantage of Max's lack of fire.

He opened up again. The range was down to less than two hundred meters now and he saw men fall. More bullets were hitting the car and steam was coming out of the barrel jacket as it heated up but Max kept up a steady fire. The second belt was running out. Max gritted his teeth. Fresh belts were down below and he would have to abandon the gun to reach them. The belt ran out and Max dove down into the car. He grabbed another belt and climbed quickly back behind the gun. As he wrenched the cover back and slipped the new belt in he could see men jump up, firing as they ran. Two bullets hit the turret in front of the gun and Max flinched. He felt rather than heard them for he was deafened from the roar of the Vickers.

Yanking back the charging handle Max started firing again. Now he was sweeping the barrel back and forth. More men fell as the range was under a hundred meters now. The first grenade arced in and exploded twenty yards in front of the car. More followed. They threw up dust and debris obscuring Max's sight lines. Soon the car would be in grenade range; then it would be all over.

Glancing down Max saw that the belt was nearly gone. He wouldn't have time to get another; the enemy would be all over him. His heart was beating as the end of the belt ran toward the gun. And suddenly all of the enemy were up and running...away. Shocked Max let off the triggers. Every enemy soldier was falling back not even bothering to fire or back away. Through the steam rising off the barrel jacket he could see they were running full out. His mouth falling open Max sagged back in shock. He had been dead, he was sure! What had happened? He stood up in the turret for a better look and it was then that the huge shadow of the Zeppelin fell over him. In shock he stared upward. L-107 was cruising in from the southeast at 1000 meters.

Max had not heard the drone of the engines because he was totally deafened. To Max's abused ears the great airship seemed to drift soundlessly across the sky. He waved and yelled knowing full well his comrades could not hear him. Hundreds of yards ahead bombs began tumbling from the Zeppelin. The enemy infantry had reached their trucks and were desperately trying to climb onto them as the trucks maneuvered. Max climbed out and sat on the edge of the roof and watched the frantic retreat.

Instead of pursuing the enemy the Zeppelin broke off its attack and circled back toward the car. It was lower now just a hundred meters above him. As it neared Max could see a line coming down with something attached. When the bundle was just feet above the ground it dropped; the line attached to it falling as well. Max jumped down and ran to the bundle. When he unwrapped it he found a K98 carbine, and canteen of water. Attached to the canteen was a paper message. Max unfolded it and read:

Max,
Friendly forces 5 kilometers south of your position. You have been on

He opened up again.

leave for too long and we expect you back at your post soon. Well done.

Trautloff

Max grinned as he took a sip of cool water from the canteen and looked up. The Zeppelin was turning north to pursue the fleeing troops. He jumped down from the car, shouldered the rifle and headed south. A half hour later he saw an armored scout car coming fast toward him. It was one of the new SdKfz 222s. The car slowed to a stop and the commander lifted his goggles and leaned down from the turret, "Leutnant Von Clausen?"

Max nodded and grinned at him.

The German soldier smiled back, "We heard you need a ride home."

Max yelled, "I sure do!" An armored door opened in the lower armor and a grinning native soldier hopped out and smiled. Max climbed up into the armored car thinking this crew was from one of one of the new mixed units the colonial government was forming. Inside Max collapsed onto a folding seat as the car rolled away. He leaned back and closed his eyes; he was safe.

A week later, Max was standing in a formation in the shadow of the moored Zeppelin. He, Wenig and Brandel stood three paces in front the assembled crew, all wore dress uniforms. They were listening to Captain Trautloff speak. As he did, Max thought about his return. The crew was happy to see him. Many had congratulated him or shook his hand. Leutnant Brandel seemed in awe of him although Max was trying to discourage any hero worship. At one point Ernst had asked him incredulously, "Did you really fly a bomb into a ship?"

Max had tried to keep his face straight as he replied calmly, "Not exactly. We just converted the cloud car into a weapon and someone had to steer it." Brandel had seemed to accept this but still seemed in awe of Max.

Wenig had been more relentless. He had spoken up in the officer's mess one night "You know Max if you spend any more time figuring out clever ways to leave the Zeppelin maybe you should transfer to the new Fallshirmjager regiment," referring to the experimental parachute unit that was being formed for commando work in conjunction with airships. That had got a good laugh from the officers present. Max's reply had been unprintable.

Meanwhile missions had continued until today when the captain had called this formation. When he finished with his short speech he marched up to Max. He reached out and pinned new insignia to Max's uniform, stepped back and saluted, "Congratulations Kapitan Leutnant Von Clausen. Max returned the salute and said, "Thank you Captain."

Trautloff smiled and said quietly, "You've earned it Max." Raising his voice he shouted out, "Ship's company, dismissed!"

As the formation broke up the captain spoke to the officers, "I need to see all of you in my office in a half hour. There's something big breaking." He nodded and turned on his heel to cross the airfield. Wenig and Brandel took turns shaking Max's hand. Wenig smiled, "I think we have time for a quick round of schnapps to wet down those new stripes, Max. We may need it if there's something big on the horizon."

Max agreed, "I could use a drink."

PART THREE

TAKING THE OFFENSIVE

It was just after 3am and very quiet in the control car of L-107. The great Zeppelin slid nearly silently through the moonlit sky over the DOA.* Kapitan Leutnant Max von Clausen always marveled how smooth most travel was in the great airship. He leaned toward the port at his navigator's station and stared at the earth passing a kilometer below. They would soon pass over Lake Manyara leaving the hilly highlands west of Mt. Kilimanjaro behind. This was not far from the uplands where Max had been stranded over a week before.

Max and L-107 were returning from a long patrol over the African coast. Most British commercial shipping had left east African waters in recent days. Mombasa harbor was almost empty when they bombed it yesterday afternoon. Now they were only four hours from their base at Tabora. He sipped from his coffee and continued to watch the passing country side illuminated by the full moon. West of the lake they would enter the deep rift country of the northern DOA.

This was the area where geologist Hans Reck had first discovered evidence of early man in 1913. His researches in the 1920s made Olduvai

Gorge a prime site for archeologists around the world. Max had read about Reck's adventures and when he had been posted here he had hoped to visit the famous Olduvai Gorge. Unfortunately his plans had been shelved when the British had decided to start the nasty border war they were now engaged in just days after he arrived in Africa.

Max shook his head. There were often incidents among the great powers that turned violent at sea or especially in their colonies but despite his four years of service, Max had not seen actual combat until this most recent series of incidents. The British had attacked German East Africa attempting to hold down German forces and keep them from interfering in Britain's lightning occupation of German Togoland in West Africa. This strategy kept German forces occupied but the British plan had not counted on the strong reaction of German forces in East Africa. With full command of the air, German forces had inflicted a series of stinging setbacks on the British forces. Ships had been sunk and German bombings had seriously disrupted British ground forces and infrastructure. Unfortunately, instead of de-escalating the conflict Britain seemed intent on reinforcing their forces and escalating hostilities in Africa. Max was worried that if someone didn't start making sensible decisions soon, there would be world-wide war between the two empires.

The young navigator ran his hand through his brown hair and raised his coffee cup to his lips. He realized it was empty and stood up to get another cup. As he did his attention was drawn to a metallic clicking coming from the radio compartment across the narrow corridor. He walked that way and came up against the captain coming aft. He gave way as the Korvetten Kapitan Trautloff turned into the radio room and listened. A moment after the clicking of the Morse key stopped, the captain stepped in the corridor reading a message. Without looking up he called out loudly, "Leutnant Wenig to the control cabin, at once!"

The quartermaster acknowledged this order as Trautloff turned to Max, "What's our position?"

Max turned and re-entered the navigator's compartment. He turned on a dim lamp that illuminated his chart. He quickly found their location and pointed it out, "Here, Herr Kapitan. Just to the north of Lake Manyara."

"Distance to Tabora?"

Max had just checked those figures, "Approximately four hundred kilometers, sir. About four hours at our current speed." The captain looked thoughtful as he handed Max the handwritten copy of the newly received message.

From Naval Air Station Tabora:
To: All East Afrikan Commands

Airfield at Tabora bombed this date at approximately 0200 local time. Moderate damage to hangars. One mooring mast out of action. Electrical power damaged. Airfield remains open. Large single enemy airship withdrawing NNE.

Max wordlessly handed the message back and picked up his calipers and a pencil. While he was bent over the map there was metallic thud forward as someone slid down the ladder into the control cabin. Moments later the tall figure of first officer Peter Wenig loomed up next to the captain, "Yes, sir."

The captain handed him the message and said quietly, "Trouble, Peter."

Finished, Max stood back from the table as the captain stepped forward. Max had drawn a line running NNE from Tabora across the frontier. As Wenig whistled softly to himself, Max pointed at a spot on the map, "We're here. The bandit was last seen along this line. Probably headed for Nairobi."

Wenig leaned in over the captain's shoulder. Trautloff spoke quietly, "We're in good position to intercept, Max. Draw up a course." Max nodded and took a seat at the table. The captain turned to his first officer, "What do you think?"

Wenig rubbed his chin, "It was bound to happen. The Tommies have finally sent some Zeppelins in. The question is how many and what class?"

The captain nodded as Max looked up, "What do you think the enemy's speed will be, sir?"

"As Peter says; it all depends on what class ship the bandit is. Most of their airships have a top speed of only 100 kph or so. If I were the bandit I'd be running at top speed for home. Use that speed, Max."

"Yes, sir."

Wenig asked the next question, "What if it's one of their new ones, sir?"

Trautloff nodded, "Their new R 80 class are nearly as fast as we are. That would be a problem."

His calculations finished Max pointed at the map, "At a top speed of 100 kph on this course the enemy should be here now. If we steer course 285 degrees we should intercept him somewhere south of Ikoma in about three hours, sir."

Trautloff nodded. He turned and went forward to give the new course to the quartermaster. Max looked questioningly at Wenig.

The first officer shrugged, "The Tommies haven't got that many zeps. Most of them are the old R 40 class. If they're serious they'll send more than one. What worries me is how many are out there."

He nodded and left, leaving Max with his thoughts. He found himself excited but nervous at the same time. He had seen enough combat in the last few weeks to realize this was probably normal. Every time they went into action, he felt the same way. He had never asked but he wondered if others felt the same way. The captain always seemed so calm and in control. If he was ever nervous Max certainly hadn't seen it. His thoughts turned to the enemy airship. L-107 had seen a lot of action in this new border war but they had not encountered any enemy airships so far. How would things go?

Three hours later Max was still thinking about enemy airships as he watched the sun break the eastern horizon. Looking down he saw the first rays of sun sweep across the open veldt. He stepped up to the captain's side and spoke quietly, "We should be cutting the enemy's track now, sir."

Trautloff nodded, and spoke aloud, "Steer 020 degrees." He turned to Max, "We'll zig zag along this course. At our speed we should overtake them soon unless it's one of their faster ships."

Max nodded and lifted his binoculars to his eyes, knowing that every free lookout on the ship was doing the same.

An hour later Max's eyes were burning from staring out at the brightly lit sky. He could feel the tension in the control car as every free set of eyes scanned ahead and to each side. He looked at the captain who was busy taking a report on the intercom. He hung up the receiver and turned to Max, "What's our position?"

Max lowered his binoculars and glanced at his watch, "Should be coming up on Ikoma soon, sir."

The captain looked thoughtful, "Distance to base?"

Max did some quick math in his head, "Uh, nearly five hundred kilometers, sir."

Trautloff nodded and moved to a bank of instruments on the bulkhead. He reached out and tapped the altimeter. He then picked up the intercom and pressed a button. A moment later someone must have answered and he gave the command, "Vent cells three, six, nine and twelve; five seconds worth."

Max rubbed his chin. He knew that as the giant airship sailed under the hot African sun the helium in the cells expanded and became lighter. This made it harder to hold altitude. The usual procedure was to carefully vent controlled amounts of helium before they climbed too high and the relief valves began calving precious helium into the atmosphere. The problem was L-107 had been in the air for nearly forty hours. There was only so much helium to vent. More important ballast must be getting low after all the maneuvering they had done, Max thought. Ironically fuel wasn't a problem. They carried enough fuel to keep them in the air for several more days. It was helium and ballast that usually ran short on long flights.

Max swung up the binoculars and again scanned forward. He was sweating, wondering if his calculations had been correct. They had been on this course for nearly an hour and should have sighted the enemy by now; unless the enemy had changed course to throw off pursuit. Or if the bandit was one of the new, faster airships that Wenig had spoken of. Or if… Max's worries were cut off by the buzz of the intercom.

Trautloff lifted the receiver and answered, "Bridge; Captain speaking." There was a pause and then he said, "Very well. Thank you." He then pressed a button on the intercom panel waited a moment and said, "Enemy in sight. I need you in the control cabin." He hung up and announced, "Forward lookout has sighted the enemy on the starboard bow at extreme range. Come around to 045 degrees."

Max moved to one side and trained his binoculars on the bearing. He could see nothing. The forward lookout was high in the nose of the ship and would have a much better view, especially if the enemy was above them. Every eye strained for a sighting. Soon Max was distracted by the first officer's figure coming down the ladder from the hull. As he hit the deck the captain gave the command, "Ten degree up angle. Steady at 1500 hundred meters." The deck tilted and Max saw it. A small black spot silhouetted against the sky at just about their altitude. The captain was climbing above them so they could see the enemy ship clearly.

As he watched, Max saw the black dot grow slowly larger. Behind him he could hear the captain and first officer speaking quietly. He listened more closely. Wenig was saying, "Ballast is low. Helium isn't in much better shape."

The captain replied, "At the rate we're closing we should be on them within an hour."

Wenig replied, "Depending on how much maneuvering we have to do, it might be hard to make it back to Tabora after a battle."

As Max listened he could see the small form of the enemy airship growing larger. Soon they would be able to identify it. They had leveled off. The enemy was now slightly below them, Max estimated its altitude at about 1000 meters.

Both the captain and first officer moved up next to Max and the three officers stared at the enemy ship through binoculars. Minutes passed before finally Wenig spoke, "I think it's one of their R 40 class, sir."

A moment later the captain replied, "I think you're right Peter. It's too thin to be one of their new ones. Max adjusted the focusing knob on his binoculars and the small silhouette became clearer. Yes, Peter was right. The enemy Zeppelin was long and thin with the center section essentially cylindrical. He had only seen photos but he knew that the newest British airships were strangely shaped. They were very fat in the middle tapering to fine points on both ends. They reminded Max of the strangely shaped ball the Americans played with in their football games. He let out a long, quiet breath. They would definitely have the advantage in speed and ruggedness in any shootout with the bandit.

Max lowered his binoculars as the captain ordered Wenig, "Get the gunners to their stations. We'll come in above and behind them. That will minimize return fire." Wenig acknowledged this order and climbed up into hull. Max pointed out to port and spoke up, "Ikoma is nearly off to port now Captain. We're only about 70 kilometers from the frontier."

Trautloff nodded, "We'll be lucky to catch them on our side. The battle could easily drag us further north as well." He looked squarely at Max, "You understand that it will be a tough trip home with our ballast and helium situation."

Max nodded, "Yes, sir." He tried to look nonchalant as he continued, "We can't let the enemy get away though. We'll just have to make the best of it." Trautloff gave out a very small smile as he replied, "Of course."

The captain gave small steering commands as they closed on the raider. Max could make out details now. The enemy was definitely an older model. It's cylindrical center section and external engine cars gave it the look of the German designs from ten years ago.

They had closed to less than 10 kilometers when the captain picked up the intercom and pressed a button. After the usual pause, Max heard him order Leutnant Brandel to the control car. Minutes later young Ernst Brandel slid down the ladder and saluted the captain, "Jawohl, Herr Kapitan."

Max tried not to smile at the young man's formality. Brandel was young and still very nervous around the captain. Trautloff looked down at the young leutnant and asked, "Is that hummingbird of yours ready to fly?"

Surprised, Brandel hesitated a moment before replying, "Yes sir, she's ready if you need her." Brandel had been assigned to them two weeks before. Along with the young leutnant had come a small, disassembled glider to be used for testing. With Trautloff's permission, Max and Ernst had removed the second glider seat and installed a radio and mounted twin machine guns in the nose. They had decided if the craft was to be tested they might was well try to make it useful. Although he had been teaching Max the basics of flight, Brandel was the only one aboard the Zeppelin qualified to fly the glider.

"Ammunition?"

"Two hundred rounds per gun, sir."

"And the radio has been tested?"

"Yes, sir."

Trautloff nodded. He pointed forward and said, "We're closing on the enemy but we are reaching critical levels of ballast and helium. It is essential that we bring him down as soon as possible or we may have trouble making it home. Do you understand, Ernst?"

Brandel answered after a moment, "I think so, sir."

"We're above the enemy. What I'm proposing is that we launch the glider now. If you can maintain that altitude or climb you should be able to make a pass from above along his full length. I don't believe he has many guns that can fire at that angle. With luck you can hole him enough to slow him or force him down." He let Brandel digest that for a moment before asking quietly, "Do you think you can do that?"

Brandel thought for a moment then asked. "What is our altitude, sir?"

"1500 meters."

"And the range to the enemy?"

Trautloff glanced forward and answered, "Less than ten kilometers."

Brandel looked out of the cabin ports to the bright sunshine outside and then spoke slowly,

"It's rapidly warming. If I can catch an updraft and soar higher I'm sure I can reach the enemy, sir."

Trautloff nodded and then lowered his voice, "You understand you'll be on your own after your attack. Ikoma is off to port. Your best bet would be to make for there and hope you can get close."

Brandel to his credit did not hesitate. He stood up slightly straighter and nodded, "I understand, sir. I'll be all right."

Trautloff nodded, "Good. Man your glider."

Brandel saluted and quickly climbed the ladder into the hull. Max looked at the captain who spoke quietly, "It's our best move at this point."

Max nodded, "He won't let you down, sir."

Lifting his binoculars Trautloff looked forward and replied, "I never thought he would."

The enemy airship grew bigger as they closed. Minutes later the intercom buzzed and the captain answered. He listened and said, "Very well. Stay in contact as long as you can. Good luck, Ernst." He turned to Max and ordered, "Max go forward and stand by the forward gun to observe. Send Leutnant Wenig down on your way."

Max nodded, "Yes, sir." Letting his binoculars dangle from his neck he moved to the ladder and began to climb. Moments later he was in the hull on the main catwalk. After the brightness of the control cabin the catwalk seemed in near darkness. As his eyes adjusted, he asked a passing crewman for the first officer. Getting directions he moved forward. He found Wenig checking one of the ballast tanks. It was always more noisy in the hull especially as they were near one of the big diesel engines mounted above and out board of them. There was a mechanic supervising it and the extended propeller shaft that exited the hull to drive the large propeller. Max yelled to make himself heard, "What's the bad news?"

Wenig tapped the gauge and yelled back, "Nearly empty. The other tanks are the same." Max nodded grimly, "The captain's launched the glider to attack the raider. I'm going forward. He wants you in the control cabin."

Wenig smiled and clapped Max on the shoulder, "Looks like another rough day. Stay low." He turned and headed aft. Max turned forward. Minutes later he was climbing the steep steps up the forward gun position in the nose.

The nose position was manned by a gunner and an observer with binoculars. The former crewman was leaning over the 20 mm MG FF. They stiffened as Max approached. Max waved them down and motioned to the observer. He obligingly moved aside so Max could take his place at the forward port. It was in the very nose of the Zeppelin above the mooring mount; Max had a breathtakingview. As he watched, the glider entered his view to port. It was perhaps a kilometer off and already slightly above the Zeppelin. Max watched the glider fly in a large circle around the bow of the Zeppelin and disappear to starboard gaining altitude. Ernst must have found that thermal updraft he was hoping for.

Max lifted his binoculars to his eyes and focused on the enemy airship. It was nearly six kilometers off at an altitude of 1200 meters. He focused and the enemy airship swam into view. It was a standard British design;

just under 200 meters in length with a semi streamlined cylindrical hull. Its five low horsepower engines could only drive it forward at just over 100 kph. It was a design at least ten years old. This class of ships was intended to be eventually replaced by the new R-80 class airships that were just beginning to enter service with the British air fleet.

They were closing slowly on the enemy but every minute of the chase drew the L-107 farther from home. It was essential they bring the bandit down quickly. Max let his binoculars dangle on his chest and scanned the sky ahead. He saw the glider immediately. It was perhaps 2 kilometers ahead now and higher than before. Evidently Ernst was climbing the thermal in large circles. When he had enough altitude, he could straighten his course and dive toward the bandit.

Max reached out and picked up the intercom phone mounted on the bulkhead. There was buzz and the line was answered almost immediately, "Bridge."

Max replied, "This is the forward lookout. I have the glider in sight, sir. He is over 2000 meters high and climbing. He is closing on the enemy and should be able to make an attack soon."

"Very well, keep us informed." The captain hung up the line and Max lifted his binoculars again. The glider was still climbing but its turning circle was smaller now. Max judged its altitude at over 2500 meters now. He looked down towards the enemy airship. Its aspect was changing. He watched for a moment and grabbed for the intercom. When it was answered by the captain he spoke, "The enemy is coming around to starboard and climbing, sir."

"Very well."

Max lowered the intercom handset and focused on the enemy. Realizing they couldn't outrun the Zeppelin the enemy Captain had decided to fight. Most of his guns would be along the lower half of the airship. He was climbing and turning trying to bring his guns to bear. His view of the enemy airship changed slightly and Max realized the captain had ordered the elevators to up. Their nose was rising as they matched the enemy's climb.

Max scanned the sky for the glider. He sighted it still climbing in great circles above them. He estimated its altitude at nearly three thousand meters. Max frowned. He didn't know what kind of ceiling the little craft was designed to have but he did know it was dangerous to fly over 3300 meters without oxygen...and the glider certainly was not equipped with that.

He estimated the altitude of the airship at nearly 1700 meters now. Using his binoculars he focused on the small form of the glider. He could see it clearly. It had abandoned its circling and straightened out. As he watched, the glider's nose tilted downward and it began diving toward the enemy airship. In a shallow dive, the glider closed rapidly with the bandit. As Max watched, Ernst pulled the now fast-moving glider out of its shallow dive behind and slightly above the airship and skimmed forward. The two mismatched aircraft were too far away to hear or see anything dramatic but Max did see one line of bright tracers arcing upward from the tail of the airship. In mere seconds the glider was past the airship and Ernst was pulling up, trading his speed for altitude.

Max grabbed for the intercom. It was quickly answered, "Bridge."

"Sir, the glider's attack looked good. There was some return fire but the glider appears unharmed. He appears to be climbing around for another attack."

"Very well."

Max returned his gaze to the glider. It appeared unharmed and was climbing in a large circle around the enemy airship. Max refocused on the enemy. Not expecting an attack from above, the enemy airship probably did not have more than one or two machine guns that could fire upward. Minutes later Max watched the glider dive in for another attack, again from stern to bow. They were closer now and this time Max could clearly see tracers reaching upward from the enemy's tail. He also caught a glimpse of tracers from Ernst's guns as he raked the enemy. Seconds later Ernst was past and climbing away. He seemed unharmed and Max let out a breath he hadn't realized he had been holding.

Refocusing on the enemy Max watched and waited as they closed slowly on the enemy. Soon he was sure that the enemy ship was sinking slightly. Ernst's attack must have holed her in many places. They were only 8 mm holes but hundreds of them along the hard to repair upper sides would take their toll on the enemy airship's buoyancy. The enemy seemed to be slowing as well.

Max reported this to the bridge and was ordered to stand by. He turned his place over to the observer and climbed down six feet to stand near the gunner as he checked his ammo belt, the large 20 mm shells gleaming brightly in their metal disintegrating belt. The gunner charged the gun and hunched over the sight. The intercom buzzed and the observer listened for a moment and hung up. He then yelled to the gunner, "Open fire when you're ready."

Looking over the gunner's shoulder Max could see they were less than 2 kilometers from the enemy and closing. The British airship was definitely lower now. Max judged its altitude at less than twelve hundred meters. L-107 was above and closing rapidly from the rear. The enemy now filled the viewport even though it was well over a thousand meters away.

The forward gun opened up with a bang. The gunner held his triggers down and hosed a long burst into the upper side of the enemy airship. Max grimaced and stuck his fingers in his ears. The gunner and observer were unconcerned. Undoubtedly they were wearing their ear plugs, something Max hadn't even thought of. Max craned forward looking over the gunner's shoulder. He could see that their speed had fallen off as they closed with the bandit. As he watched, tracers from the 20 mm arced down and into the hull of the enemy. Other streams of tracer from lower in the Zeppelin's hull were also converging on the enemy. It was taking a pounding, absorbing hundreds of small shells. Answering fire came from only one gun mounted in the tail of the British airship. Their other guns mounted lower on the hull could not be brought to bear. They were more than six hundred meters above the bandit now closing very slowly on it. At that moment the forward gun fell silent. The gunner immediately began reloading the gun with a fresh belt of brass cartridges. Looking back outside, Max was surprised to see they were turning away to starboard. The bandit was definitely sinking now with a tail down attitude. Tracers continued to arc out from the Zeppelin as they came around on a parallel course. Reloaded, the nose gunner again opened fire again. Now he was arcing the gun around to port as they came along the bandit's starboard side eight hundred meters away.

L-107 had been sinking parallel to the enemy. They were again down to about 1000 meters; above and off the enemy's starboard side now. At least half a dozen streams of tracer converged on the bandit's engines. From his position Max could see only two tracer streams arcing up from the enemy. Her nose was coming up as the enemy commander went to full power on his engines and full up on the elevator. Still the bandit's tail continued to drop; it was perhaps only five hundred meters above the African veldt.

Certain that the enemy was finished Max climbed down from the gun position and made his way aft toward the control car. As he dropped off the ladder into the car, he immediately looked for the enemy airship. In the time it had taken for Max to reach the control car the Zeppelin had circled off to starboard of the enemy and slowed until it was barely moving. Their guns had fallen silent. Whether they had been ordered to cease fire or whether the gunners could see that the enemy airship was doomed Max didn't know. The captain was in the radio room. As Max moved up next to Wenig and raised his binoculars, he could see the enemy was very low now. It was still desperately trying to gain altitude as it skimmed, nose high, barely above the ground. The African veldt was fairly level in this area, the great plain broken only by brush and the occasional huge acacia tree. Ahead and below the doomed airship a large herd of giraffes broke and ran in all directions as the huge shadow swept over them. Max watched as the large enemy ship sank lower to the ground. Suddenly he saw a plume of dust thrown up from the tail as it dragged along the veldt.

The enemy airship pitched down violently. Unfortunately the ship's duralumin frame couldn't take the strain of the violent twisting of the airship. Max watched in amazement as the enemy airship split, just aft of the midships engines. The aft section slammed hard into the ground. The forward section of the airship, still attached at a few points pivoted slowly, the nose of the airship reaching upward until it finally pointed up at perhaps seventy degrees. Max imagined the chaos aboard the enemy airship. The crew must be clinging to anything solid to prevent themselves from being thrown aft. Meanwhile equipment torn loose and anything not secured would be raining aft, tearing through the already strained framework. At last the duralumin frames connecting the two sections snapped and the aft section slid to a halt, clouds of dust swirling up along its path as it left a trail of fabric and metal on the ground behind it. Fabric peeled back in huge sections flapping along the ships flanks. As it came to rest the frame partially collapsed as the weight of the tons of unsupported duralumin pancaked downward. Free from the dead weight of the aft section Max thought for a moment that the nose section would float free.

Something like that had happened to one of the early American Zeppelins ten years before. Torn apart in a violent thunder storm, the nose of the American Zeppelin had free ballooned for several kilometers before coming gently to earth in an orchard. Unfortunately this crew was not so lucky. Heavily holed as well, the nose section did not gain altitude. It skimmed nose high along for a hundred meters before the dangling wreckage at the open end caught in a large tree. Max stared as the nose fell rapidly downward as if the entire forward section of the airship was a tree falling in the forest. It slammed hard into the veldt throwing up a large cloud of dust. It must have made a hellacious noise but here a thousand meters in the air it all happened in silence. Max felt a sadness come over him as he stared at the wreckage of the huge ship. Strangely, he hoped the giraffes had all managed to escape from under the descending airship.

Wenig spoke quietly, "My God!"

The enemy ship was in two sections. The nose had come to rest at a ninety-degree angle to the stern; about a hundred meters separated the two sections. As the dust settled Max could see small figures emerging from the hull sections and fleeing in all directions. Max didn't want to think about the airship's control car now buried under tons of duralumin in the forward section of wreckage. He hoped its occupants had abandoned it before they hit.

The captain loomed up behind the two officers, "I just spoke with Brandel. He's unharmed. He says the glider took some minor damage but is still controllable. He is making for Ikoma. I've ordered the radio to alert our garrison there to look out for him."

Max nodded to himself as he continued to stare at the wreckage of the enemy. He was glad Ernst was all right. He lifted his binoculars and counted more than twenty small figures gathering in groups around the downed airship. It looked like a lot of the enemy crew had escaped unharmed. Behind him, the captain gave calm commands to the helmsman to circle the wreckage. Max's feelings were mixed. They had pursued and caught the enemy. They were no longer a threat to German forces. But he was shaken at watching the enemy airship die. He couldn't help but think that that was how they would look if they crashed. Max shook his head to clear it and moved toward his navigator's station to plot a course for home.

The crew of L107 fought an increasing head wind as the ship flew south for home. The sun was just setting as they finally came in sight of the Tabora airfield. After being in the air for over fifty hours, and fighting a running battle, the officers and crew were tired. The only interesting thing that happened on the trip home was a discussion the captain started with his officers. He had asked them for their opinions on the use of the glider. High command would certainly want to know about its usefulness. Wenig had been thoughtful, "I don't know if this was exactly why they sent it out here but it did come in handy. I guess those modifications that Max and Ernst did came in handy." He paused for a moment, "It's dependent on weather though. If there are no updrafts the glider can't say aloft for very long."

Max added, "It certainly looked impressive climbing up and then

…the nose fell rapidly downward…."

diving on the enemy. Ernst then used his speed to climb back up for a second pass. With the second seat removed and no observer the glider easily handled the weight of the guns and radio."

The captain nodded, "I agree; the glider was useful. I'll make a positive recommendation in my report." He moved off and Max mused aloud, "I'm surprised no one's used gliders like that before."

Wenig shrugged, "Too dependent on the weather. No wind, no updrafts and a glider can't fly very far."

Max looked thoughtful, "Maybe, they need to be powered. An engine would give them all the lift they need."

In reply the first officer shook his head, "It's been thought of before. I've read articles in several flight journals over the years. The problem is weight. You assembled our glider, Max. It's way too fragile to carry a heavy, water cooled V8 or V-12 diesel engine."

"How about a light weight engine; maybe something air cooled."

Wenig shrugged again, "Nobody's built engines like that for over twenty years. Everybody's building big, slow turning engines for Zeps and blimps. Besides you'd have to beef up a glider frame and that means even more weight. You'd need a perfect balance of a light weight engine with plenty of horsepower. Plus you'd need a light but strong airframe."

"I suppose you're right. It's too bad though. If our glider had power it could fly out far ahead of us and really increase our scouting range. Not to mention giving us an additional weapon against enemy Zeps."

As Wenig turned away he said smilingly, "It would revolutionize vehicles too. Diesels are good for trucks and our armored vehicles but think of what small, lightweight engines would mean for autos. The builders would probably fill the roads with so many cars you couldn't get anywhere."

Max turned back to his chart table to check their course back to Tabora but the idea of powered gliders hovered at the back of his mind for a long time.

L-107 tied up at the remaining undamaged mooring mast just after sunset. As the captain ordered the engines shut down and the crew landing stations Max stood up from his table and stretched. After two days in the air it would be good to be on solid ground again.

Fifteen minutes later Max was standing in front of the damaged hangar. Upon landing the captain had immediately headed off toward base headquarters. The first officer was busy giving orders about refueling and maintenance work. They had emerged nearly unscathed from the brief battle with the enemy airship and should be ready for another patrol within hours. The crew was another matter. They were all ordered to stand down for rest. Too wound up to sleep, Max decided to look around.

Damage from the bombing was obvious. There were several craters in the tarmac around the other mooring mast and it was obvious it had taken at least one direct hit. The steel frame was damaged, with bent and broken beams that were being swarmed over by ground crew. Max could even now see the too bright flicker of acetylene torches cutting away damaged framework. He skirted several more craters in the smooth tarmac before he came to Hangar One. It had been hit by three bombs. They had left fairly small holes through the curving metal roof. The light-weight aluminum covering had not been hard enough to detonate the bombs. Instead it looked like all three bombs had plummeted through and exploded on the hard concrete of the hangar floor. The bombs had damaged a lot of equipment and caused several casualties. Max could see small holes in the hangars walls from shrapnel. He could also see blood stains on the concrete. He passed out positive words to the repair crews he came across. In return, he answered more than a few questions about the battle with the enemy raider. An hour later he managed to get back to the officer's quarters. He found Wenig in the small common area sprawled out in an easy chair drinking beer from a bottle. Max waved and headed for his room when the leutnant called out to him. He stopped as Wenig sat up saying, "They picked up our intrepid pilot."

Max turned, "Ernst? Is he alright?"

"Looks like it. Forces from the garrison at Ikoma picked him up outside of town. He's probably at the officer's club right now, regaling everyone with exciting stories. Lucky dog!"

The last word they had received from Ernst was that he was attempting a soft landing in a flat area just outside of town, "And the glider?"

"I didn't take the call but the captain said it was only lightly damaged. I guess Brandel will be back in a couple of days if he can commandeer a truck and help to load the glider."

Max was relieved. He had been stranded alone out in the vast Africa veldt and he didn't envy Ernst walking home as he had been forced to. Before heading for his bunk, the tired leutnant asked Wenig, "Anything else going on?"

Wenig drained the beer bottle and stood up, "Captain said to get some rest.

There's apparently something 'big' in the wind. He wants to see us tomorrow at ten sharp." Too tired to ask more about whatever 'big' meant, Max nodded and headed for his room. Inside he jerked of his boots, threw his tunic onto a chair and collapsed onto the bed. He was asleep within seconds.

The next morning both Wenig and Max stood before the captain's desk in his office. They were both in clean uniforms and alert. Max had slept well but the continuing flight operations and stress of missions was beginning to tell on him. Inside he was bone weary. A good night's sleep had helped but he reflected he need about a week of those...and no flying. All he seemed to think of nowadays was fuel loads, weather reports, intelligence reports and bomb loads. He snuck a covert look at Wenig. The first officer seemed his normal cheery self. He, like the captain never seemed to be worried or tired. He was always ready with one of his smiles or sardonic comments. Max wanted to shake his head. Would he ever look cool and rested all the time? Maybe that was it took to be a commander? If so, he had a long way to go. He tried to look alert as the captain stood up, "We did good work yesterday. The admiral sends his compliments to the entire crew. That goes for you two also." He paused as his two leutnants nodded then continued, "Pass that along to the crew. Meanwhile new orders have come down."

"The admiral has been working with Naval Airship Command on a big plan. Reinforcements are arriving very soon and we are going to be part of a new offensive." He walked over to the large map of Africa on one wall and looked critically at it for a moment. He then turned and said, "The two of you see to the ship today. I want it fully ready in thirty hours for extended flight. Give the crew what rest you can but see that we are fully ready to lift off by tomorrow afternoon."

Both officers nodded. Before he could speak Wenig asked, "What bomb load, sir?"

Max was shocked when the captain calmly replied, "No bombs. We're going out unloaded."

Inside Max was as surprised as he knew Peter must be, but trusting the captain implicitly he did not ask the obvious question but instead inquired, "Will Leutnant Brandel be back with the glider by then, sir?"

The captain turned and replied calmly, "That is unknown at this time. I have spoken with the Leutnant and he hoped to have the glider disassembled and on a truck by tonight. Apparently, it was only moderately damaged.

It is unlikely he will be back before we lift off tomorrow. Regardless, we could not take the glider with us anyway. His orders are to return here and prepare the gilder for flight. He will rejoin us hopefully at a later date. Is there anything else?" The two leutnants remained silent, "Very well. You have your orders. Lift off tomorrow at 1600 hours. Dismissed."

The two officers saluted and left the office. In the hall headed outdoors Max asked, "No bombs? What do you think's going on?"

Wenig thought for a moment, "I'm not sure. Even on a long recon patrol we should have some armament. And why are we prepared to leave Brandel and the glider behind? All I can think of it must be a long trip where weight is important. Maybe we've been ordered home?"

Max was startled, "Do you think so?"

"No, but we must be going somewhere where weight is more important than bombs. Forget that for now. You scrounge up a couple of mechanics. Run up each engine, check everything; power, seals, oil consumption, everything. I'll double check fuel, gas and ballast. After that I'll get a crew to climb up and double check every cell for leaks?"

Max nodded, "Right," and headed off toward the crews' quarters.

Exactly on time the next day, L-107 cast off its moorings and slid into the hot afternoon sky. The captain had indicated he wanted both his officers in the navigator's cabin. As expected, Ernst had not returned by lift off time. He was still somewhere north of Tabora with the glider loaded on a truck. Once they were safely off the ground and cruising at 1000 meters headed south southeast the captain came aft to the navigator's cabin.

Keeping his voice low he spoke quietly, "I'm sorry to keep you two in the dark but our orders are top secret. We can't let any wind of this reach the Tommies. Surprise is crucial. As you can tell, our course is straight for Dar Es Salaam. We will slow and loiter once we get there. We must land no earlier than 2000 hours. At the airfield outside of town we will rendezvous with L-102 and a third Zeppelin. There, all three Zeppelins will take on full loads of combat troops that have been quietly assembling for over a week. These are Fallschirmjager from the new regiment who have been flown in at night on several supply flights."

Ignoring the surprised expressions on his officer's faces he continued, "Once loaded we will transport the troops to an inland drop zone on the island of Zanzibar. We will then return for another load of troops.

Altogether the three ships will put down over six hundred fully armed troops. They will move before dawn and attack the town from landward. At dawn the East Afrika Squadron accompanied by most of the destroyer squadron from Dar Es Salaam will cover the landing of more forces at the edge of the harbor. Zanzibar harbor is empty as you well know. We have driven all British shipping out and isolated the fort and garrison."

"At dawn the three airships then will land three hundred troops on Pemba island to attack its garrison. After all troops are landed, we will all return to Dar Es Salaam and load bombs. Orders are to provide air cover over the landings and shadow and attack any British ships that attempt to intervene from Mombasa." He looked from Wenig to Max and back. Max was at a loss for words. Not so Wenig, who wryly commented, "It's about time. Zanzibar and Pemba have been a thorn in our side for decades. They properly belong to the DOA anyway."

Trautloff smiled slightly as he replied, "The High Command thinks so too. I understand that the Kaiser himself has approved of this invasion."

Max finally spoke, "It doesn't make up for their sneak attack on Togoland but I'm with Peter!"

"Good. When we get to Dar Es Salaam, you two will be in charge of loading the troops. You will also fly inside the hull keeping an eye on them. I don't want anybody falling off a catwalk and out through the ship's hull. And there will be a lot of weapons around. Make sure nobody shoots anyone. Clear? Good. Any questions?"

"How about navigation, sir?"

"I'll handle it. Zanzibar's not far. I can't miss that. L-102 dropped in an advance party last night by parachute. They have located an isolated clearing inland. They will mark the landing zone and act as a ground crew. We will get in fast and unload as quickly as possible. We will be number two. All right; to your stations."

Wenig spoke, "C'mon Max. Let's check the ladders and ropes." Trautloff nodded as the officers headed for the ladder into the hull.

Five hours later L-107 was easing down in the darkness toward the dim lights that marked Dar Es Salaam airfield. Max was watching out an open hatch in the lower hull. The night was dark. What little moon there was would not rise until an hour before dawn. Lights were few on the airfield. No doubt because of the possibility of British airship activity. Still, Max could make out the large shadowy shapes of two other Zeppelins separated by some distance and moored at masts. Since there were only two masts, L-107 would moor in the open steadied by nearly a hundred ground crew, manning the lines.

They were barely moving forward across the tarmac at minimum altitude when the order came to drop lines. The crewman next to Max dropped a coil of rope through the hatch and then kicked a wooden rung rope ladder attached to the frame after it. Max pulled on his gloves and waited. The great airship moved at a walking pace across the tarmac. As the engines were cut back to idle, dozens of ground crew holding the lines took up their slack. Max didn't wait for the Zeppelin to come to a complete halt. He grabbed the line, wrapped his legs around it and slid out through the hatch, six meters to the ground.

On the ground in the dark shadow of the huge ship he pulled a flashlight from his pocket and turned it on. He then began yelling orders to the ground crew. Gradually the ship was pulled down until the control cabin bumper was just brushing the ground. This still left the belly of the Zeppelin three meters above him. Other rope ladders were already being unrolled through every available opening in the ship's lower hull. The cargo platform was also being winched down.

In minutes the ship was stationary and ready for boarding. Max waved his flashlight at the mass of soldiers lined up in the darkness. They came trotting up and immediately began climbing the ladders into the ship. He could see a file of soldiers lined up at the short boarding ladder to the control car to enter through there. Max turned at a yell from a familiar voice. He saw Leutnant Wenig standing next to the lowered cargo platform. He was waving men forward with a flashlight. Heavily burdened soldiers lumbered forward dropping their loads onto the platform. Sailors from the Zeppelin immediately began stacking the cargo.

It seemed confusing but Max could see that loading was going well. The officers assisted by flashlight wielding sailors were shouting, pointing and even pushing soldiers to where they needed to be. As soldiers brushed past him toward the rope ladders he flashed his light over them. Each soldier wore a helmet and carried a rifle slung across his back. But there was something odd about their helmets.

Max focused his light on a climbing soldier. His grey coal scuttle helmet was shorter than normal. It looked as if the flaring rim had been trimmed back. Over their field gray uniforms each soldier was also wearing a loose, camouflage smock that hung nearly to their knees. Max could see the hump of small packs each soldier wore under the smocks. This was new. Max wasn't up on all army protocols but decided the camouflage might work very well on the heavily vegetated islands of Pemba and Zanzibar.

Twenty minutes later the last soldier was aboard. Max, still on the ground, watched as the cargo platform was raised into the ship's hull and then confirmed that every rope ladder was pulled into the ship as well. When everyone was aboard, he trotted to the control car. The captain was standing in the open hatch. Max saluted, "All troops aboard. Ready for departure, sir."

"Very well." The captain leaned forward, his hand out stretched. Max took it and pulled himself into the control car. He brushed past the captain who was closing the passenger hatch and made for the ladder into the ship.

Once in the hull Max found mass confusion. There were soldiers everywhere. They were crowded along every catwalk and packed into every nook and cranny. He could only make his way aft by calling out, "Make way!" every few steps. As he moved he cautioned soldiers to watch their footing and try to stay out of the way of crewmen. Still making his way aft Max felt the increased vibration of the engines and knew they were lifting off. Even heavily loaded the Zeppelin still moved smoothly into the air. Finally Max reached the cargo area. Wenig was supervising sailors tying down their rapidly loaded cargo.

The platform was covered in wooden crates, 50 mm mortars and MG 34 machine guns. Max could read the contents of the crates stenciled on their sides; 8 mm cartridges, 50 mm mortar bombs and hand grenades. It certainly looked like the Fallshirmjager had come ready to fight. Max got up close to the first officer and raised his voice, "Well, that went pretty well."

"So far. We've got to keep a close watch on all these soldiers though. Scattered all over the hull if they move around too much it'll throw off our center of gravity. Go back forward and keep an eye on things. Hopefully nobody will drop their rifle through the hull." Max nodded and moved forward.

Zanzibar harbor was only a hundred kilometers north of Dar Es Salaam and the trip should have been a short one but Trautloff took them out to sea and came in across the darkened island from the east. The journey only took an hour and a half but it seemed longer to Max. Moving among the nervous soldiers he urged them to keep calm and not move around. Loaded for combat the soldiers were clumsy and sure enough one of them dropped his rifle. It bounced off the main catwalk and clattered through the duralumin framework before going through the fabric hull covering barrel first. Max heard the commotion and shoved his way through the soldiers and airmen to where sailor was shining a flashlight downward through the frames. Sure enough there was fist sized hole in the hull with darkness on the other side. At the hedge of the hole pieces of fabric flapped back and forth. Max gritted his teeth. Until they could patch it from the outside the hole would only get bigger. The faster they flew the faster the tear would grow. Unfortunately there was nothing to do now. They would just have to hope for the best.

Finally a sailor grabbed Max's arm and shouted he was wanted on the intercom. He worked his way to a hand set and spoke into it, "Von Clausen."

The captain's calm voice replied, "Max we're closing on the landing zone. Stand-by to disembark."

Max acknowledged and sent a crewman to alert Wenig. He then worked his way to a hatch and opened it. Rushing air boiled up from the darkness. He bent over the opening but could see nothing but blackness. The night was dark. Moonrise wouldn't be for quite a while. Craning his head to one side he saw a light on the ground to one side. This gave him an idea of their height. He could also feel the Zeppelin slowing. They were still more than twenty meters high but moving forward barely at all. Max kicked the coiled rope through the hatch knowing that other landing lines were going down as well.

A moment later the vibration of the engines decreased. The captain had cut all of them to idle. Now it was up to however many Fallschrimjager were on the lines to literally pull them down. His flashlight pointed down Max watched the ground inch closer. All he could see was tall grass below. When they were seven meters off the ground he grabbed the line and slid to the ground.

Max found himself standing in knee high grass. A quick sweep of his flash found nothing bigger than chest high bushes near him. He signaled upward with the flashlight and stepped back. It was a good thing because seconds later a soldier slid down the rope. He released it and moved off into the darkness unslinging his rifle as he moved; more quickly followed. Unloading went faster than loading. The Fallschrimjager ignored the rope ladders and slid quickly down the lines. Around him at a distance he could see flashlights waving, guiding the arriving troops away from the Zeppelin. Seeing the soldiers needed little help, Max moved to the cargo platform and helped unload equipment. He quickly grabbed crates and handed them to waiting soldiers who disappeared in the darkness. Soon the platform was empty and Max hitched a ride as it lifted into the ship. He then moved aft making sure all lines were being pulled in. Soon he felt the increased vibration from the Zeppelin's engines as she launched upward.

The return journey was quick and smooth. Max's only duty was to report the hole in the hull to the captain who had acknowledged it without comment. At least it hadn't been a soldier Max rationalized to himself. By midnight they were back at Dar Es Salaam. There it was the same organized confusion. Still, the loading of over a hundred soldiers in near darkness went just as quickly. This time Max made a point of grabbing a Fallschirmjager officer and pulling him aside. He recounted the lost rifle story and warned him to stay on top of his men. The young, fit looking leutnant nodded and said he would before scrambling up into the ship. The only other thing Max did while on the ground was to search the ship's lower hull until he found the hole. It was bigger but not huge. Max could only shrug and move on.

The second flight to Zanzibar was just as short and as agonizingly long as the first trip. They managed to easily find the darkened field. There were more flashlights moving about on the ground and that helped. They landed safely and began immediate unloading. Max again was the last man aboard as they lifted into the darkness. Max congratulated himself as they climbed to altitude. At least they hadn't put any more holes in the hull.

By 2:30 am L-107 was landing once more at Dar Es Salaam airfield. They took on board their final load of troops in less than an hour and were soon in the air headed this time for Pemba Island. Pemba, north of Zanzibar was smaller and less heavily garrisoned. It was also hilly and heavily vegetated. They approached from the steep eastern side of island and cruised down the spine of hills that ran north to south along the entire length of the island. Half way along the ridge of hills, opposite the lights of town on the west coast, they finally saw the dim lights of the marked clearing. Max was at a lower hatch peering down waiting to kick out lines as they descended. It was incredibly dark below and his only reference were the dim flashlights held by men on the perimeter of the clearing which seemed awfully small to Max's eyes. The airship was moving slowly forward at near walking speed as it dropped lower and lower. Suddenly a darker mass passed just under the ship. Before Max could shout out a warning there was a shudder from the tail and a large ripping sound. They had come in too low and scrapped through a tree or trees. He stood up and began squeezing past bodies towards the tail. He met soon met Wenig coming the other way. He shoved a soldier to one side and shouted in Max's ear, "We tore up the tail. I don't know how badly. We have to get these men off and check damage from outside." Max nodded and turned forward again.

By the time Max again reached the open passenger hatch they were slowing. The lines were down and unseen hands were attempting to stabilize the great airship. The engines went to idle and the noise level dropped considerably. Max kicked out the rope ladder and motioned the closest soldier forward, "Go, go, go!" he yelled. Soldiers crowded forward and the chaos began.

Max squeezed into line and was the third man off. He immediately dodged to one side to keep the next soldier down the rope from landing on him. He quickly oriented himself and used his flashlight to gesture men off to the left and right. As he directed traffic in the near darkness popping noises came to his ears. He tensed; that was small arms fire in the distance. It was scattered and at some distance but it still worried him. The attack wasn't supposed to go in until dawn. Had surprise been lost? Whether it had or not Max still did not envy men flailing around in the dark shooting at each other. He had had some experience with ground combat and knew first hand that it was terrifying in daylight when you could actually see what you were doing much less fighting in the dark. It was times like this when he was thankful he was in the navy.

When the last soldier had dropped off the ladder and disappeared in the darkness, Max ran aft flashing his light along the belly of the airship. Other than the still fairly small hole he saw nothing until reached the lower tail fin. He found Wenig already there staring upwards. Max immediately saw the problem. They had clipped the top of some large, unseen tree in the dark. There were more than a dozen tears and rips in the fabric covering the fin. None were particularly large but the longer they flew the bigger they would grow. As the two officers moved aft they flashed their lights on the moveable rudder attached to the fin. Max heaved a sigh of thankfulness when they could find no damage to the important lower rudder. Shaking his head Wenig spoke, "Well, let's go break the news to the captain." They turned and made their way forward under the great airship toward the control car.

Minutes later they were reporting to the captain. He listened to their news and thought for a moment, "We can't stay here to make repairs. We don't have the proper scaffolding. We'd have to jerry rig ropes for the repair crew and that would take forever. Also this place could easily be a battle zone in a couple of hours. We'll have to chance further damage to get back to a proper base." He shook his head, "Damn! We'll be needed over the battles for support at dawn but I'm afraid we're going to be late. Take your stations, gentlemen. We have to go." They saluted and headed to their places for lift off. Minutes later they were high in the concealing darkness headed for friendly territory.

They moored to a mast at Dar Es Salaam airfield an hour before dawn. The captain immediately jumped to the ground and walked toward the headlights heading their way. Wenig needed a certain amount of the crew to load bombs as quickly as possible. Max grabbed every other crewmen not needed and organized them into repair crews. They armed themselves with fabric, large sail needles and heavy thread. Others carried cans of heavy dope to paint the patches once they were sewed on. In fifteen minutes Max had his repair crews assembled under the tail awaiting portable scaffolding. He paced impatiently but was forced to wait ten more minutes for the first trucks to arrive. Base repair crew jumped off the flat-bed trucks and began handing aluminum tubes down to the ground. The airship crewmen pitched in to help and in minutes the aluminum tubes were being assembled into frames that went up around the damage tail. The bottom of the tail stood about two meters of the ground. Some of the rips were three meters above that.

As fast as the frame work went up, crewmen climbed up to whatever damaged spot they could reach and began their work. Directing his men, Max's attention was diverted for a moment as trucks pulled up beneath the airship and armorers began unloading bombs. The 50 kg. and especially the 100 kg. bombs needed multiple men to carry them to and place them carefully on the cargo lift. As soon as the platform was loaded it lifted into the belly of the ship where Wenig oversaw their placement in the bomb racks.

Things were very busy for a while. Max did not neglect the now meter sized hole in the lower hull where the soldier had lost his rifle. He soon had two men stretching canvas across it. The captain came by and gave some encouragement to the men and then made himself scarce. His officers and men were well trained and knew their business.

The crews had been at their work for nearly an hour and it was going well. Max moving back and forth on the ground supervising the repairs was aware of the gradually increasing light. It was still before sunrise but the sky was growing lighter by the minute. This helped speed up repairs and he was glad of the coming dawn but he was also terribly aware that the main landings were now beginning on Zanzibar and Pemba and L-107 was not there to support them.

More concerning was the reddish gray light that lit up the eastern horizon. Clouds had moved in overnight. It seemed to be a light overcast but it signaled a change in the weather. As he turned back toward the ship the tall figure of the first officer appeared sliding down a rope from the ship's hull. Wenig hit the ground lightly and walked over to Max, "How's it going Max?"

"Pretty well, we're nearly finished. All the bombs aboard?"

"Loaded and ready." He pointed to the east, "I see we're in for some weather."

Max's reply was cut off as both officers caught a drone on the light breeze. They stepped out from under the shadow of the Zeppelin to watch the other Zeppelin coming in. Max immediately saw that it wasn't one of the civilian supply Zeppelins that he had halfway expected. It must be L-102. The huge ship was perhaps a hundred meters up and moving toward them at walking speed. As it maneuvered toward the nearby mooring mast its long flank was revealed and Max realized something looked out of place

Instead of the familiar silhouette of L-102 Max saw a brand new Zeppelin silhouetted against the false dawn in the east. The new airship wasn't be much bigger that L-107 but Max did see not the usual three extended propeller shafts running down the side of the hull he saw four. The control car under the nose also was bigger and so were the tail fins. And in the lower tail fin, just ahead of the black and white painted iron cross, Max could see windows and men moving inside them.

Next to his shoulder the first officer spoke, "It's about time we got some help around here. I'm getting tired of carrying the whole load ourselves."

Nonplussed Max exclaimed, "You knew about this?"

Wenig nodded, "She brought the last load of Fallschirmjager in yesterday. I heard about it last night from a Captain that went in with the last load of troops. I guess the High Command has decided to get serious about pushing back the Tommies."

Max could only breathe out, "She's beautiful."

"I agree. L-139, first in her class; just completed her trials. For once something went right for a change."

"She's got eight engines!"

"Right; and they run on the new Blau Gas that everyone's so excited about. It's supposed to make ballast problems a lot easier."

Max replied excitedly, "I've heard about that. It's a gas fuel that doesn't displace any more than air. As it burns you don't have to vent gas to maintain your altitude." His mouth turned downward at the corners, "Wish we had engines like that."

Wenig clapped him on the shoulder, "They'll probably be refitting all the Zeps eventually. C'mon let's go report." The two officers turned toward the control cabin to see Kapitan Trautloff walking toward them. The two officers stiffened to attention and saluted. Trautloff returned the salute and asked, "How's the loading going Peter?"

"All bombs aboard and loaded into the racks. Full load, sir."

Trautloff nodded and turned to Max, "And the repairs?"

"Completed, sir. The dope won't be dry for a couple of hours and they're not too pretty but I think they'll hold."

"We don't have time to wait for them to dry. We are launching immediately. Good work you two. Let's get aboard." He turned and walked forward his offers close behind.

Minutes later the ship was ready to launch. This time Max was at his navigator's station. Wenig stood near the captain. Trautloff gave the command, "Schiff Hoch," the engines went to full power, the ground crew dropped the landing lines and L-107 rose smoothly into the sky once more.

Sunrise was minutes away as they climbed away from the airfield.

An hour later L-107 was approaching the harbor at Zanzibar. Through his binoculars Max could see smoke spiraling up from multiple fires burning in the small city. In the harbor he could see several warships. Flashes from their decks showed they were firing at targets ashore. The great airship drifted in slowly. Soon they could identify the warships as German.

The captain cruised over the contested city at two thousand meters. Visibility was not good. Light rain was just starting to fall. A destroyer was alongside the quay and was unloading troops. Once ashore the soldiers immediately moved out into the streets. Max focused his binoculars on the city. He could see troops moving through the streets and obvious combat. If he looked closely he could make out the lighter khaki of the colonial troops and their Askari auxiliaries. This distinguished them for the darker feldgrau clad German regulars that had recently been airlifted into the colony. There was certainly heavy fighting in the city but there were no obvious targets to bomb and he was not sure exactly what they could do to assist the troops. The captain must have agreed because he spoke aloud, "I think the Army has the situation in hand. We'll leave the ships to give them support Make your course 010; engines to full." Max nodded as they turned north away from the harbor. Looking down Max could see the British cruiser they had bombed next to the sea wall. Its deck was awash and it was obviously abandoned. Spoils of war Max thought. Perhaps the Germans could raise it if they took the island.

They turned northward for British territory fighting a head wind and increasing rain. An hour and a half later the Zeppelin was approaching Mombasa from the southeast. They were at 1000 meters approaching from the sea. It was still raining and the ship was heavy. To maintain altitude Captain Trautloff ordered ballast dropped. Max focused his binoculars forward on bright flashes near the coast. As he focused the image came into view. A ship was firing its main guns. Max recognized the cruiser *Darmstadt*. She was a new, fast mine-laying cruiser that had been assigned recently to the East Afrikan squadron. She was one of the first of a new class of ships popularly known as "colonial cruisers" intended for overseas service in Germany's colonies. She must have been sent to mine Mombasa' harbor.

Max refocused his binoculars on the *Darmstadt's* target. It was a British destroyer that had just cleared the harbor and was standing out to sea at high speed. He could see the tall splashes of shells exploding around the enemy ship. There was a flash as she replied with her own deck guns. Max felt the captain move up next to him, "We won't waste any bombs on her. Let's see if there's any worthwhile targets in the harbor."

Max nodded and shifted his position to the opposite side of the control car as the Zeppelin came around to port. Soon they were crossing the southern headland and the shallow southern channel. Mombasa was built on an island at the mouth of two shallow rivers. The harbor was on the north side of the island. The old colonial fort was there as well as the more modern seawall. Max swept his binoculars across the harbor. Several buildings were burning along the waterfront. Smoke drifted over the small city. He could see a half sunken freighter in the middle of the harbor. Another was aground across the river on the north bank of the river. It had obviously been bombed and was listing heavily to port in the shallow mud flat it was aground on. "We got that one last week," Max thought to himself. Other than a few fishing boats and other small civilian craft the harbor was empty.

He turned as the captain ordered a course change to the south. The Zeppelin came around over the harbor and headed south across the city. There were several fires burning in the city as well. Held down by the

...they could identify the warships as German.

rain the smoke was clinging sullenly to the rooftops of the city obscuring many of the streets. The city was still occupied Max could see. The streets were crowded with people, carts and wagons. There even trucks fighting through the crowds filling the streets. But Max noted, there were no guns firing at them at all. Surprised he asked the captain, "Have the British abandoned the city, sir?"

Trautloff looked thoughtful as he replied, "After Zanzibar they must think we're going to invade the city. It's possible the military forces have withdrawn inland, Nothing here worth attacking." He lowered his binoculars and looked at Max, "It might be better to follow that destroyer. It must be going somewhere, after all." The captain gave orders and they circled over the city and out to sea. As they passed just south of the harbor entrance, they saw that *Darmstadt* had broken off pursuit of the enemy destroyer and was now laying mines across the harbor entrance. Focusing his glasses Max could see the black mines falling through doors in the cruiser's stern and into the water. Every few seconds an ugly black cylinder would fall from one of the doors into the water, immediately sinking below the surface. As they passed over the cruiser at full speed, Max could see a blinker light flashing from the cruiser's bridge upwards at the Zeppelin.

At nearly 120 kph it did not take long to catch up to the fleeing destroyer. As they came up on it, tracers arced upwards. The captain had expected this and the ship was now at 2000 meters and the tracers fell below the ship. At this altitude visibility across the sea was not good. The rain continued to fall. Despite its coating, the fabric covering of the great ship absorbed moisture and the sheer amount of water sluicing across and off the enormous surface of the Zeppelin made it heavy and difficult to handle. The captain had been forced to drop even more ballast as they pursued the fleeing enemy.

They paced the destroyer; three kilometers behind and two thousand meters above it as it ran at full speed east southeast. Within an hour of catching up to it, the captain took a call from the forward observer. He listened a moment, thanked the lookout and turned to Max, "Forward lookout reports flashes in the mist, barely seen off the starboard bow. Range perhaps five kilometers. It seems our friend has led us to battle. Better check your sight, Max."

Max saluted and moved to the bombsight near the rear of the car. He quickly checked it over and reported back to the captain. Looking out the nearby port he could now see the flashes ahead. It was still raining and visibility was poor but soon the darker shapes of warships could be seen through the mist. Then Max saw it; a dark gray shape passing through the clouds ahead three kilometers in front of them. It was there, then quickly gone in the clouds. Max called out, "Zeppelin ahead!"

The captain did not seem surprised, "That'll be the L-139. 102's south of Zanzibar scouting." He turned and entered the radio room for a moment. Moments later he returned and had the helmsman slow the ship. Moments later the radio operator called out, "Message from L-139!"

The captain returned moments later, "Somewhere below us are two enemy cruiser s and as many as three destroyers. They are on a course southwest headed for Pemba Island." "What's left of their east African forces," thought Max. The captain turned to Max, "With this cloud cover we need to see what's below us. "

Max nodded, "The Cloud Car, sir?"

"I'm afraid so. Keep us informed. We'll bomb when we can hope for a lucky hit. Our main job is to slow them up and keep them off balance until more of our forces come up." Max saluted and headed for the ladder into the ship.

Ten minutes later he was in the car and being lowered below the Zeppelin. Max had on a heavy leather jacket and goggles but it was still wet in the car. When he reached the full extent of the cable he found himself still in the clouds. Giving commands over the telephone he had the captain gradually bring the ship down to 1500 meters. That left him just below the cloud level at 800 meters altitude. Max immediately sighted an enemy ship off to starboard. He gave commands and L-107 came around.

The enemy was a destroyer moving southwest according to Max's compass. It was making good time, Max judged; twenty knots or more. Knowing the chances of a hit were slight Max brought the Zeppelin, hidden in the thick clouds above, in across the destroyer's course. As they passed in front of the ship Max gave the command to "drop." Eight fifty kg bombs spilled out of the clouds exploding in a line a hundred meters in front of the fast moving ship. Alerted by the bombs the destroyer's light guns opened up on the Cloud Car. It wasn't the first time Max had been under fire in the car. He stayed calm and called the ship asking to be reeled in two hundred meters.

At that altitude he was actually flying in the lowest clouds. As he sailed in and out of the gray mist he was mostly invisible but could still keep an eye on the enemy. They continued to shadow the destroyer they could see. Max was wet and becoming chilled but he stayed with it calling out course corrections and observations.

Half an hour later, the telephone buzzed. Max answered and found the captain on the line, "How are you doing, Max?"

"Fine, sir. It's a little wet down here but I'm managing."

"I'm sorry but we can't get down low enough to sight the enemy without endangering the ship."

"It's all right, sir. Next time we'll have Ernst aboard and I'll get to stay warm."

The captain laughed. As junior officer it would normally be Ernst's duty to man the Cloud Car on missions of this type. Max was about to say something else when he spotted a ship emerging from the mist off to starboard. He immediately called out, "New ship in sight." He lifted his binoculars and focused through the mist. The image swam into view and Max realized it was an enemy cruiser. He called it in and the captain brought the Zeppelin around toward this new target.

Max conned them into the same attack position as before. They came in across the cruiser's path. As Max called out the drop the cruiser sighted his cloud car and opened fire with light guns. It also turned hard to starboard. Max stayed calm as tracers lanced through the clouds around him. He concentrated and clearly saw their salvo of bombs drop just off the port side of the now turning cruiser. The closest bomb landed a good forty meters away from the enemy but it still must have worried them for the enemy ship continued into a 180 degree turn and ran into some low-lying mist.

This was the pattern the Zeppelin and its crew followed for the next two hours. Whenever Max sighted a ship they attacked. No hits were recorded but each time the enemy was forced to turn or retreat into clouds and mist. Meanwhile the captain continued sending out reports to direct German surface ships closer. Max was by now so chilled and wet that his teeth were chattering. He picked up the telephone to ask the captain for another observer to replace him when he caught sight of another enemy ship. The captain answered but Max frowned, wiped his goggles and stared at his compass. Finally he heard, "Cloud Car, report. Are you all right?"

"Sorry, sir. I've sighted another ship…but it's headed north, sir."

"North? What's its speed?"

"It's moving quickly, sir. At least twenty knots."

"Stand by."

There was a pause. Max pushed his gloved hands under his armpits to keep them warm while he tried to figure out how he could be this cold in Africa. Finally the phone buzzed. Max grabbed it and the captain spoke, "Max, I've just spoken with L-139. They've also been tracking and bombing a cruiser for nearly an hour. No hits; but the cruiser turned north a few minutes ago and is holding the new course."

"What do you think, sir?"

"I think with their ships spread out in the bad weather they hoped for surprise but that is lost with us tracking them. I believed they have decided to withdraw. We'll stay with them for a while to see if it's just a feint. But you've been down there long enough. I'm bringing you up for a rest. Someone else will take a turn."

Max hung up the phone and leaned back as he was reeled up into the clouds. It would be good to be warm again. Once back inside the Zeppelin Max took the time to change clothes and get some coffee before he reported to the control car. Once there the captain patted him on the shoulder, "Good job, Max."

"Thank you, sir. But we didn't get one hit in six separate attacks today."

"No matter. We convinced the enemy to turn north. We've protected our landings and that's what we set out to do. It looks like the enemy has withdrawn, at least temporarily." He turned away and Max made his way to the navigator's table. He sat down and let out a breath. It looked like the landings had worked out well enough. But the British wouldn't take the losses well. What would they try next?

The room was tall and finished in dark hardwoods. Paintings of sea battles and famous admirals, some over a century old, decorated the walls. Tall windows spanned the width of one wall. The light they provided was dull and gray and they were streaked by water from the rain beating against it. A long, polished oak table occupied the center of the room. Several men sat around it. Two wore sober civilian clothing. Most wore dark blue uniforms that could barely be recognized behind the gold braid and colorful ribbons. The distinguished, gray-haired admiral at the head of the table looked down the length of the long table at a younger counterpart, "Admiral Smart do you have the latest summary of the situation?"

The shorter officer stood with dignity and replied, "I do, First Sea Lord." He placed a set of spectacles on his nose, carefully picked up a sheet of paper from the table in front of him, cleared his throat and began, "The garrison at Zanzibar surrendered to German forces this morning at 0700 hours local time." There was slight stir from among the men surrounding the table. The admiral then continued, "We have had no contact from our forces on Pemba Island since yesterday. At that time they reported that resistance was continuing but was scattered and apparently less that effective. They also requested any naval assistance possible."

One of the other admirals asked, "And what naval assistance do we have available?"

Admiral Smart removed his glasses and set them on the table, "Unfortunately we do not have any forces that can intervene in time to be of any help."

The First Sea Lord frowned from the other end of the table, "Surely our forces in East Africa are quite close. Can nothing be done to reinforce the Pemba garrison?"

"Yes sir, we do have considerable ground forces scattered from Nairobi to Mombasa. But unfortunately there is no way to get them to either Pemba or Zanzibar."

Another officer spoke up, "But what about the East African squadron?"

Admiral Smart replied slowly, "If you have been reading the dispatches, you know that the East African squadron has been heavily engaged the last few weeks. One cruiser now rests in shallow water in Zanzibar harbor. I'm afraid the Germans own that one now. Another cruiser has been damaged so badly that it was forced to withdraw to our base at Aden. It reached there three days ago." He picked up another sheet of paper, "The reason that it had to withdraw was that the harbor at Mombasa is unusable. Harbor facilities have been bombed almost daily for the last two weeks by German Zeppelins. I had a signal from the commander of the cruiser squadron yesterday that he is also withdrawing north to Aden with his remaining ships." He dropped the paper on the table, "Apparently we lost another destroyer while attempting to support the Zanzibar garrison. Other ships have been damaged. He reports Mombasa is unusable as a base at this time."

He sat down is face still and hard, "The truth is gentlemen; we have temporarily lost control of East African waters."

There were looks of surprise and disbelief on several faces. The First Sea Lord at the other end of the table asked quietly, "And German losses?"

"Over the last three weeks of battle our forces have claimed four German destroyers sunk and damage to at least two of their cruisers. They have also claimed several hundred miscellaneous casualties, mostly ground troops." He looked down and cleared his throat before adding, "And of course, regrettably the odd few civilian casualties."

One of the civilians with a thin sour looking face fixed the admiral with a scowl, "Why admiral, are our forces not able to cope with one small cruiser squadron?"

"I'm afraid Minister that the Germans have complete command of the air. Their Zeppelins give them a big advantage in reconnaissance and intelligence. They have also been heavily bombing our harbors and keeping our ships from refueling and replenishing."

"And what about our own airships?"

"You are aware Minister that we lost the R59 five days ago?"

"Yes, I am. As is every British taxpayer who can read a newspaper. The uproar in Parliament is deafening. The opposition is demanding an inquiry into the conduct of this uh...this uh...situation." The gray haired First Sea Lord knew why the Defense Minister hesitated to use the word 'war' but he held his tongue. Meanwhile the Minister had turned his glare on him, "First Sea Lord, what are our plans to retrieve this situation?"

The First Sea Lord replied carefully, "We have ordered *Chatham* and *Devonshire* to Aden from Bombay to rebuild the East Africa squadron. Destroyer forces are being shifted from the Med but that will take time. We have other plans afoot but they also will take time to mature. I am afraid Minister, that for the time being we must accept German dominance of the African coast"

The Minister looked as if he had swallowed a lemon, "The Prime Minister will not take this well." The other men around the table all stared in any direction but at the Defense Minister. Finally one of the other officers cleared his throat and asked, "Uh, what about Force J?"

The First Sea Lord looked down the table at the short admiral. Admiral Smart spoke carefully, "It is still forming. We are awaiting reinforcements from the Atlantic. We hope it will be ready to sail in a few days."

"Troops?"

"Elements of the 2nd South African Division and all of our own 3rd Infantry division are available for loading."

"What about co-ordination with our forces in East Africa?"

"Uh, as you are aware First Sea Lord, direct communications with Nairobi and Mombasa are out. We are relaying commands through Cairo and Khartoum but that is uh...cumbersome. However, General Hawthorne in Mombasa is aware of the plan and claims he will be ready."

The Minister spoke up, "Why, admiral, is direct communication not possible?"

"I'm afraid Minister, that the radio mast at Nairobi was destroyed by bombing two weeks ago. The smaller mast at Mombasa was destroyed six days ago."

No one else had anything to add or perhaps no one wanted to hear any more bad news so the table fell silent while the minister fumed. Finally he stood up. His aide stood up as well and reached for a briefcase. The Minister spoke, "Thank you First Sea Lord. I will report the current situation to the Prime Minister. I'm afraid he will not be pleased. Good day, gentlemen." He turned and left the conference room his aide close behind him.

As the door closed behind the minister and his aide, The First Sea Lord looked out the window at the rain and said so quietly that he could barely be heard, "He's not the only one."

PART FOUR

DECISION IN AFRICA

The three officers stood in the early morning light flooding the airfield at Tabora and watched the huge silver shape of L-139 climb slowly away. She was a beautiful sight; the reddish early morning sunlight reflected off her tail surfaces and turned her silver hull to the color of molten gold. The youngest of the three, Leutnant Ernst Brandel, watched her departure and scratched his chin thoughtfully as the drone of its eight powerful engines began to fade, "She's not circling. She's headed west."

The tallest of the three, Leutnant Peter Wenig, executive officer of L-107, turned to their third companion, "You know Max, I believe our junior officer is correct. That is west, isn't it?"

Leutnant Max Von Clausen nodded sagely, "Since the sun definitely rises in the east every single morning, I believe Ernst has it correctly. 139 is definitely headed west. I knew he would pick things up quickly out here." Knowing his fellow officers were having a little fun at his expense didn't stop Brandel from blushing slightly, "But she's supposed to take the next sea patrol out eastward. She's headed inland."

Slightly surprised himself, Max shrugged, "Must have gotten last minute new orders. That's the problem in the navy; nobody bothers to tell us leutnants anything. What do you think Peter?"

Wenig shook his head, "I'm as surprised as you. I thought she was headed out to patrol north of Mombasa. Something must have come up. I'll bet the old man will know. If something's happened he'll be calling for us soon anyway."

The three turned and started walking across the tarmac toward the officer's quarters. They were officially 'off duty' today. They had just returned from a two-day flight patrolling for nearly fifteen hundred kilometers along the East African coast searching for signs of British naval activity. In the six days since the capture of Zanzibar and Pemba islands, the three German Zeppelins assigned to the DOA had been running almost continuous patrols north and south along the coast expecting a naval response from the British.

L-107 had returned from such a patrol the night before. The crew had been given a day to stand down. They were scheduled to go out on patrol again the next morning. The third Zeppelin, L-102 was even now patrolling somewhere off the African coast. As the officers neared their quarters an enlisted sailor rushed out the door. He seemed quite surprised to see the officers. He saluted and said, "Kapitan Trautloff's compliments and he wants to see the three of you in his office in half an hour." Max's comment as the three officers returned the man's salute and pushed past him into their quarters was, "There's that call you were talking about, Peter. Special orders it must be." The pleased sailor headed off toward the mess hall. He had been lucky to find all three officers almost instantly. Now with time to spare, a cup of coffee seemed like a good idea.

A half hour later all three officers stood in Kapitan Trautloff's office awaiting his pleasure. The tall, distinguished officer spoke, "Stand easy, men." The three officers relaxed slightly. Trautloff continued, "By now you know that L-139 is not going out on coastal patrol. New orders came early this morning. A British airship bombed the radio mast outside of Doula in Kamerun last night. L-139 has been sent to patrol over Kamerun until further notice." Seeing the looks on his officers faces Trautloff matched their seriousness, "Yes, I'm afraid the Tommies have sent in another Zeppelin."

Wenig queried, "Any word on what class, sir?"

Max was wondering the same thing. Taking on one of their older Zeppelins like the one that L-107 had destroyed ten days before was one thing. Taking on one of their new faster ships was something else.

The captain shook his head, "Nothing definite. Reports are still being evaluated but I wouldn't be surprised if it's one of the new R-80 class ships."

Max figured his expression probably matched everyone else. The German forces had been fighting this brush fire war for nearly a month now and there seemed to be no end to it. Every time they countered British incursions successfully, the British threw something new in. If he wasn't so worn down by the constant flying and fighting he might have the strength to get angry. The British had started this latest round of madness with the invasion of German Togoland. The Germans had countered and in retaliation captured Zanzibar and Pemba. A lot of the men, including Max, had hoped that might give the British pause and encourage them to stop things from getting more out of hand.

Max knew everyone else in the room felt the same so he kept his thoughts to himself and tried to look positive. He snapped back to attentiveness as Trautloff continued, "In light of this new development the Admiral has given us a new assignment." He stepped around his desk to the large map of Africa on one wall. He turned and spoke again, "Tomorrow morning we will leave on patrol as usual but instead of a two-day patrol south through the Mozambique Channel and return, we will continue south. He stepped up to the map and put his finger on the channel between Madagascar Island and Africa and drew it south, "We will patrol south along the coast searching for British warships. We will proceed to Durban and scout that harbor at a distance. Then we will proceed all the way to Cape Town and scout that harbor as well." As he spoke, the captain moved his finger along the coast all the way around southeastern Africa to Cape Town.

He then turned and finished, "We then will return the way we went. Naval intelligence is worried about a build-up of shipping in South Africa waters. If there is, it is almost certain to be pointed our way. It is our duty gentlemen, to find out what is going out there so we can be prepared for the next British thrust."

Max heard Ernst sigh quietly. Yes, the strain was starting to get to all of them. Max frowned and spoke up gesturing at the map, "With your permission, sir?"

Trautloff nodded. Max stepped up to the map and measured distances with his eyes. He did some quick math in his head and turned to the captain, "Sir that must be at least 4500 kilometers...one way. Round trip that's even longer than the supply missions that flew down to Africa from Europe during the Great War."

Trautloff let a small smile momentarily crease his face before nodding, "Yes gentlemen, we will have the honor of flying the longest Zeppelin combat mission in history. But it is well within range of our ship and within the capabilities of the best crew in the Naval Air Service. I have full confidence in you all. Any questions?"

Wenig let out an almost silent whistle. Trautloff again stifled a smile, "Any other questions?"

Brandel clear his throat, "Uh, we'll be carrying a full load of fuel and everything else, sir. Are we taking the glider?"

"We are. It might come in handy if we need to scout from a distance or are attacked." He looked soberly at the young officer, "You understand what that might mean Ernst?"

Ernst nodded, "Yes, sir."

"Good, anything else?"

Wenig spoke up, "Full fuel and ballast of course, sir. But what about bomb load?"

"Full load, Peter. We don't know what we may find out there. We can always jettison bombs if necessary. As for fuel we will top off on the Rufiji River before we head further south." He raised an inquiring eyebrow but there were no more questions, "Very well. Give as much of the crew rest today as you can. But see that the ship is ready for launch at dawn tomorrow." The three officers saluted and filed out of his office.

Once out in the hall Wenig spoke, "Max, take a couple of men and check over the engines. Ernst, take a couple aircraft fitters and check all the gas cells. Check every one for leaks. I'll see about fuel and ballast. It looks like there's no rest for us today." Max and Ernst turned and headed for the outside door. It was going to be a busy day.

"Schiff Hoch!" Captain Trautloff gave the command and the helmsmen moved their control wheels accordingly. The engines went to two thirds power and L-107 slid forward into the cloudy African sky. Max glanced out his viewport as the Zeppelin cleared the heavy cover of forest along the Rufiji River. A loop of the brown water in the river came into view. L-107 had covered the 1000 kilometers down to the navy's Rufiji River base in just over eight hours. They had quickly refueled and were now on their way again. Now Max would earn his pay. Over water in bad weather, navigation would mainly be by dead reckoning. He might be able to get fixes using RDF (Radio Direction Finding) but he had to hope for clear weather so he could get accurate fixes for the sun or stars.

A half hour later they were over the Indian Ocean headed south southeast at 800 meters altitude. The captain would have preferred a higher altitude so they could better scan the ocean for ship movement but they were held to this altitude by heavy clouds. Their speed was 120 kph but they were zigzagging in wide arcs to increase the amount of ocean the lookouts could scan.

Max stayed at his navigator's table, checking his charts and periodically tuning his RDF toward Dar Es Salaam which he used this as a check on their course. The weather slowly deteriorated and about the time Max took over command the rain began. On long flights like this the captain could not stay in the command car constantly. Typical procedure was for each officer to take a two-hour watch in command of the Zeppelin until relieved by another officer. Max took over from Wenig at 1800 hours. The sky was so dark when the rain began that he never saw the sun go down. He just observed the gray sky get darker until full blackness over took the ship.

Max's watch was unremarkable. Unable to see anything the great ship cruised southward. Her lookouts still kept a sharp eye below but visibility was marginal with clouds and moon rise not until early the next morning. Below the sea was dark and ominous. Ernst took over at 2000 and Max found a bunk in the hull of the ship. It was noisier in the hull. Engine vibration and the constant light flow of air through the hull almost negated the smooth ride of the Zeppelin. Almost. Max still fell into a deep sleep almost immediately.

His second watch that began at 0200 was also quiet. The rain had stopped. Max noted the ship was heavier from the accumulated moisture. He hesitated to drop precious ballast; instead he ordered increased power to the engines to maintain altitude. He caught one direction fix from Dar Es Salaam and figured they were fairly close to course.

Relieved by Ernst at 0400, Max had only been asleep for less than an hour when he was awakened by a sailor with a flashlight, "Sorry, sir. You're wanted in the control car."

Max acknowledged this and quickly pulled on his tunic and felt boots. He made his way forward and slid down into the control car minutes later. Ernst was talking quietly to the quarter master. Seeing Max he moved over and said quietly, "Sorry, to wake you Max, but you said you wanted to be called if the weather cleared. Take a look." Max stepped to the large starboard window. The only illumination in the car was dim red light so that the crew's night vision would not be compromised. It took only a few moments for Max to see that the sea was dimly illuminated 800 meters below. The clouds were breaking. Max turned and smiled at Ernst, "Thanks, this is just what we need." In the navigator's compartment he quickly swung a leather case over his neck and one shoulder to hang at his side. Into his pocket went a pencil, paper and a pencil flashlight. He nodded to Ernst as he climbed the ladder back into the hull.

Once in the hull Max made his way along the main catwalk to frame number 7. There he located the ladder and climbed up between gas cells seven and eight. It was nearly dark in the space between the cells. Only dim emergency lights lit the space between the enormous gas cells. Just enough light so that Max could climb upward. Surrounded by the cylindrical cage that encircled the ladder, Max wasn't worried about falling. The cage was broken only at intervals by openings that led out into crawl spaces for the ship riggers to inspect and repair the cells.

Max climbed all the way to the top of the hull. At the upper catwalk that ran the length of the ship, suspended from the upper keel, he stepped off and then climbed a short nearby ladder to stand on a platform that was illuminated by comparatively bright moonlight. Standing upright on the platform, Max's head protruded through a Plexiglas dome a meter across. Looking up Max could see scattered clouds above and a quarter moon low in the sky off to port. Reaching to his side he opened the leather case and pulled out a sextant. Holding it one hand he looked out at the sky and quickly located three prominent stars. He took his sightings, noting down the figures on the paper from his pocket. Nodding to himself he replaced the sextant in its case and climbed down from the platform.

Minutes later he was climbing down the ladder to the control car. He nodded to Ernst on his way to the navigator's station. Max was an experienced navigator and soon had their position carefully figured and charted on the navigation plot. They ship was in the middle of the Mozambique Channel closer to the African coast than they should have been. They had probably made their turn to the south too soon. Headwinds must have slowed their speed.

Max called Ernst over and showed him their exact position. He then told him to pass on the information to the captain when he was relieved. Then giving out a large yawn he headed back to his bunk.

The weather the next day was greatly improved. High clouds covered much of the sky and they were still getting a strong wind from the south but visibility was much greater. This allowed the captain to take them to 1500 meters and allowed the lookouts to cover a much larger swath of ocean. They passed through a couple of minor rain squalls that did not last long. The main concern was the head winds the ship was fighting. The captain was forced to run the engines harder to maintain schedule.

By 1800 hours that day, as the sun was setting the Zeppelin was about 400 kilometers east northeast of Durban South Africa. Max had gotten an accurate noon sight and was sure of their position. Captain Trautloff was pleased. At the cost of some fuel he had kept them on schedule. He ordered a course change to the west searching for Durban.

After dark it turned out that Durban was easy to find. They saw the lights of the port from fifty kilometers away. At his plotting table Max shook his head. Although men were dying in East Africa the rest of the world wasn't interested. Even the nearest large British port wasn't bothering with a blackout. Sometimes Max did not understand this state of perpetual 'semi-war' the great powers found themselves in. After the Great European War many people had decided the carnage had been too costly. Instead the Great Powers had replaced open conflict with this state of perpetual hostility. Max wondered just how many men had died in the endless round of border incidents, unacknowledged sea battles and hostile incursions. A man was just as dead in some obscure border shooting as in battle during a real war.

Trautloff gathered his officers, "This will be a quiet reconnaissance. We have the wind behind us. We'll go in high and drift over the port. No flares. Instead I want each of you to find a place to look over the port area through binoculars. We'll compare notes afterward. If we have to take further action we'll decide then. I hope to do the same tomorrow night at Cape Town. Questions?" There were none and the officers scattered to positions around the ship.

The captain brought the ship in from the east at just over 3000 meters. He had idled engines 3 through 6. With engines one and two at one third power along with the onshore wind they drifted nearly silently over the South African port at just after 2300 hours.

On his stomach in the hull, Max stared down through his binoculars at the brightly lit city. The harbor was darker than the city but he could still make out such landmarks as the light house marking the harbor entrance on a spit of land to the south east side of the main channel. The city itself lay on the north shore of the bay. The docks were well lit and Max could make out two merchant ships tied to the quay. There was no activity around them. He also sighted another merchant ship anchored in the middle of the bay. There appeared to be a number of small boats pulled up along small piers on the south side of the bay; fishing boats Max decided. The only sign of military activity he saw was a large patrol boat or small destroyer just leaving the harbor. Its narrow silhouette and relatively high speed helped the identification.

Soon enough, the Zeppelin was past the city and drifting out over the darkened country side. The captain brought it around slowly to the southeast and headed out to sea once more. The officers then gathered once more in the control car.

"Did anyone see anything that I didn't," asked the captain?

Wenig shook his head, "No, sir. Only a few lonely freighters and no military activity at all." Max and Ernst nodded in agreement. The captain smiled, "Well then, there's no use hanging about here. Max put us offshore 100 kilometers and set a course for Cape Town. Keep that distance from the coast. I want to bring us in to Cape Town late tomorrow night. Cruising stations, Gentlemen. I have the bridge." The other officers saluted and left the car. Max moved over to the plotting table and went to work. Fifteen minutes later he had a chart plotted. He fetched the captain and went over the course carefully, "We are here, sir. Roughly eleven hundred kilometers from Cape Town if we stay off shore and approach it from the southeast. At our current speed, even if these headwinds persist we should be over the harbor by noon local time. To approach sometime after midnight I propose we fly farther off shore, reduce speed and zig along the course I have marked. It will save fuel and let us scout a lot more ocean. Most importantly it lets us loiter until late at night."

Trautloff studied the chart for a moment and nodded, "Good work, Max. I'll leave the course headings with Peter at 0200. You better get some rest if you can. Your watch is in two hours." Max saluted and headed for the hull.

The next 24 hours passed smoothly. Off shore the Zeppelin zigzagged southwest at 80 kph for ten hours. The weather continued to be good. There were scattered high clouds and the ever present wind, now coming from the southwest, but they were not concerned with speed. Off Port Elizabeth they came around on a westward course. They had seen a few individual ships at a distance; freighters and one large liner headed eastward off East London but no warships at all.

Headed west along the busy shipping routes between Port Elizabeth and Cape Town the captain turned the ship farther out to sea and climbed to 2500 meters. Any ship they sighted they steered away from, staying just within visual sighting range to identify it. They sighted several freighters and another large liner most headed westward but still sighted no warships. The weather stayed good although the wind, now from the west increased. Navigation was easy. Max got a good noon sight and was able to fix their

At his plotting table, Max shook his head.

position exactly.

As the sun neared the horizon ahead of them the captain stopped at Max's plotting table to inquire about their position. Pointing to a spot on the map he replied, "Just about here, sir. Approximately 100 kilometers southeast of Cape Agulhas."

"How far to Cape Town?"

Max glanced at the chart, "Approximately 400 kilometers, sir."

The captain looked at his wrist watch and said, "About five hours at our current speed." He thought for a moment and nodded his thanks. Leaving he moved forward and gave orders to the quarter master to bring them around twenty degrees to port. He also gave orders to slow the Zeppelin. Max frowned as he looked back at the chart. The captain was circling out into the Atlantic. He must have a plan in mind.

At 2000 that night there was an officer's meeting around Max's plotting table. The captain pointed out their current position, "We are here; southwest of Cape Town. I intend to approach from the northwest at 2600 meters. We'll use Table Mountain to mask our approach. Once past it we will cut our engines and let the onshore wind push us over the commercial harbor to scout for shipping. Then we will turn south and cross over False Bay. The naval base is at Simons Town on the south side of the bay. If there is some kind of naval build up; I believe we'll find it there. We'll cross the bay quietly. If we spot any significant activity we'll come around for another pass and drop flares." He looked at Max, "If that happens I want you activate the cameras, Max. Photograph everything you see. Peter, I want you to stand by the bomb racks for targets of opportunity. Ernst you will handle the bomb sight. Any questions?"

"When do you plan on going in, sir?" The captain answered the first officer's question, "0430 hours just before dawn." He could see by the looks on his officer's faces that they needed elaboration, "Attacking so late is risky but after the reconnaissance I want to head north to the airfield northeast of Cape Town. We need to see if the British have reinforced their blimp squadron. We'll need light to find it quickly. One quick pass there and we'll head east to the coast, then north for home." He waited but there were no further questions. The officers dispersed to ready the ship.

Max looked at his wrist watch; it was just before 0430 hours; an hour and a half to sunrise. From his position looking out the view port near the navigation table he could see the silhouette of the famous flat topped Table Mountain silhouetted by the lights of Cape Town. Cape Town was situated on a large T shaped peninsula located at the extreme southwest point of the African continent. Table Mountain occupied the crossbar of the T running more or less north and south. Cape Town itself was located along the upright of the T facing north onto Table Bay. Simon's Town was located on the other side of the peninsula on the south side of False Bay.

The Zeppelin was flying at 2000 meters southwest of Table Mountain. The captain was using it to mask their approach. Behind him, Max could hear the gunners talking in low tones. The rear gun was always manned on missions. The other two gunners, standing by with their MG 15s, were waiting the call to move forward and mount their guns in windows on each side of the control bridge. The captain was busy maneuvering. Max felt the nose of the great ship rise slowly as they climbed. They would fly out into the Atlantic, turn east and cross over Table Bay and the harbor at 2600 meters with their six engines at low power allowing the prevailing wind to push them quietly over Cape Town and across the peninsula to False Bay.

As they climbed, Cape Town came into full view. It was a good-sized city and was well illuminated even at this early hour. When they were 10 kilometers west of the city the captain gave his command and the ship came around to the east. Max focused his binoculars out the port forward toward the city shore and harbor. The captain was doing the same on the port side and Max knew that somewhere in the ship Brandel and Wenig were likewise engaged.

The engines were throttled back and the city gradually grew larger. Light was low in the harbor. Finally, Max could focus in on the docks. He saw several freighters moored there and what looked like a large tanker anchored offshore. At one pier two large commercial liners were moored. The docks were mostly dark with little activity. Max felt relieved. He didn't like bombing targets close to civilian areas. Gradually the harbor slid under the nose of the control car. The captain lowered his binoculars and called out quietly, "Anything, Leutnant?"

"No, sir. No warships in port and no unusual activity. I did see a large tanker anchored in the harbor."

The captain nodded and stepped to the intercom. He picked up the handset and spoke for a few moments. When he hung up the handset he ordered, "Starboard thirty degrees." He turned to Max and said, "Max, I want Brandel on the bomb sight. You go forward to the nose and call out any targets. I expect we will see more on the other side of the peninsula." Max saluted and climbed for the ladder into the hull.

Once inside it didn't take long to find Ernst and the first officer checking the bomb racks. He passed on the orders. He then made his way forward to the lookout station in the very nose of the ship. Once there he took the observer's place and scanned ahead. There was a lightening on the eastern horizon. In an hour the sun would climb above the heights to east of the large bay. Focusing his binoculars Max swept them forward to where scattered lights ended at the edge of False Bay. He felt a rising excitement.

Minutes passed. Max raised his sights and focused on the lights of Simon's Town naval base perhaps 10 kilometers to the south, across the bay off their starboard bow. The naval base was brightly lit and even at that distance he could see many ships tied to its piers. Max grabbed for the intercom. There was the usual buzz and then the captain's voice answered, "Bridge, Captain."

"Sir, I have unusual activity at the naval base, twenty degrees to starboard."

"Yes...I can see the lights. Do you see any ships?"

"Yes, sir. Several ships at the piers under the lights. I can't...Uh, hold on, sir." Max had seen something else. The quarter moon high overhead didn't provide much light but enough to reflect off something in the bay. Max refocused his binoculars. Almost instantly a large shape swam into view. Keeping his eyes to the glasses he pulled the telephone to his ear and called out, "Sir, I have a large warship anchored north of the naval base. It is very large. I believe it's a Battleship. Wait! I have another ship anchored nearby and...Cancel that. I have one, two, three—uh—many ships, repeat, many warships anchored in the bay, including two very large warships."

The captain replied calmly, "Very well, get down and set the cameras on automatic. Then get back to the control car."

"Yes, sir." Max quickly abandoned his place to the normal observer and climbed down to the main catwalk. There he ran aft until he came to an illuminated ladder. He climbed down onto a very small platform near the ships outer covering. Kneeling down he reached down past the two large black cameras mounted to framework and slid open a port in the bottom of the hull directly under the two cameras. Cold wind whistled through the port. Max had checked the cameras earlier, so he knew they were working correctly. He flipped two switches on each camera and scrambled back up the ladder to the catwalk.

As he ran forward he was passed by Wenig and several sailors of the bomb crew headed for the bomb racks. Max reached the control car ladder and quickly slid down it into a conversation between the captain and Ernst, "With the bombs we have, we can't do much damage to the battleships, Leutnant. But we can hit those transports and dock facilities. We'll come in from the north and bomb in salvoes as we cross the port. We'll then come around and make another pass south to north. I doubt we'll have many bombs left after that. Questions?"

"No, sir." Ernst saluted and headed aft to the bomb sight. The captain turned to Max, "Cameras running?"

"Yes, sir. They'll take a photo every fifteen seconds until they run out of film."

"Good, stand by the flare launcher. Give me one every minute on my command."

Max saluted and moved to the rear bulkhead where he opened a panel, armed the flare launcher and grabbed hold of the handle. He was standing next to the starboard ports and could look out. Behind him the captain ordered a turn to starboard. As they came around to the south Max could look down and see dim moonlight reflected on the dark water of the bay. Ahead he could see the bright lights of Simon's Town docks. The British wouldn't be loading ships all night long unless it was important. And those ships could only be headed for only one place when fully loaded.

The captain called out for half speed on all engines. As the quartermaster shifted the throttle indicators, the captain turned to Max, "Stand by." Max nodded and grasped the flare release more firmly. The captain called out, "Two minutes," and leaned toward a view port. Then he turned and nodded at Max, "Flares!" Max pulled the handle hard and released it. He held his wrist watch up and watched the second-hand sweep around.

The handle released a parachute flare from beneath the control car. There a dozen such flares were mounted. The flare dropped from the bottom of the control car, the small parachute deployed and the flare burst in eye stinging brightness below the Zeppelin. With one hand on the handle and one eye on his watch Max risked a quick glance out the side. Far below he could see the harbor thrown into bright relief. They were just passing over a large ship that Max quickly recognized as a battleship. Other warships were anchored about the bay. Drifting in high and nearly silent, they had taken the British forces by complete surprise.

From aft Max heard Ernst call out, "One minute!" A glance at his watch told made Max to tighten his hold. Ten seconds later he pulled the handle releasing his second flare. Max felt his heart beating loudly in his chest.

The flares would alert the British. They could expect anti-aircraft fire at any moment. Max heard the call, "Coming up on target. Thirty seconds."

Looking ahead Max could see the lights of the first docks disappearing under the nose of the control car. He looked at his watch; another twenty seconds. Seconds later a heard Ernst call out, "Drop, drop, drop!"

The ship was far too large for Max to feel anything as the first bombs fell free. He glanced up from his watch and saw the captain speaking into the intercom headset. The helmsmen were concentrating on keeping the ship steady. The quartermaster was staring hard at the engine instruments. Max risked a quick look downwards. The brightly lit ships and piers were quiet for a moment then he was surprised to see the first of a series of bright flashes hit the nearest ship. More flashes followed along the pier. A quick glance at his watch and Max released another flare. Somewhere above, Wenig and his crew were releasing more bombs in a pattern the captain had ordered. Max heard a yell from aft. Was that Ernst? He smiled.

They were fully over the base now and Max could see they were approaching the low range of hills south of it. Moments later Max released another flare. As he did the captain order all engines to full ahead and then turned to Max, "Cease flare release." The captain then called out clearly, "That looked good. Helm to full port. Bring us around back the other way quarter master." He picked up the intercom handset and spoke to someone. Max leaned his face against the Plexiglas and looked down and aft. The base and piers were brightly lit from the sinking flares and now from several fires. As the ship turned in a huge invisible circle in the darkness Max could feel the excitement from the bridge crew.

Minutes later they were approaching Simon's Town base at half speed from over the low hills to its southwest. The panoramic view spread before the Zeppelin was entrancing. He stepped up next to the captain and stared down. There were several fires burning around the base. A large fire seemed to be spreading along one pier. Max could see at least six transport ships tied up along the docks. One was burning amidships. The flares dropped over the bay had burned out but their light was unnecessary now. It was easy to locate the warships from the pillars of white light from their reaching searchlights. Tracer fire arced upwards into the darkness; a lot of tracers. The captain spoke quietly without turning his head, "Stand by flares."

Max moved to the aft panel and grasped the handle. Moments later the captain spoke loudly, "Flares at one-minute intervals. Now!"

Max pulled the handle and raised his watch arm. Seconds later Ernst called out from aft, "Thirty seconds to drop!" The captain picked up the intercom and waited. Moments later the command came, "Drop, drop, drop."

The bombs fell. Max launched the next flare. He craned his head for a quick look out the port. Below he could see more explosions and fires along the piers and among the docked ships. Seconds later they were out over the bay. Max felt the control car jerk. Moments later it jerked again as another shell exploded somewhere below them. They were above the flares and their altitude must hard to judge by the enemy. The British were probably putting up a blind barrage along a path in front of the falling flares hoping for a lucky hit. They sailed on for another two minutes Max dropping flares accordingly until the captain turned and gave him a wave.

Releasing the handle Max stepped to a port and lifted his binoculars. They were over the middle of the bay still headed north. The last of the British warships were falling behind the Zeppelin. The captain called out, "Secure from bombing!" He then picked up the intercom to talk to someone in the ship. Max felt someone at this side and lowered his binoculars, "Well done, Ernst. We got some solid hits back there."

The young leutnant looked a little shaky but gave Max a weak smile and a nod. He pointed out to starboard, "Just in time. It'll be dawn soon." Max looked to the east and agreed. The sky was definitely lighter in the east. The sun would soon crest the distant hills.

The captain turned to them, "Well done, Ernst. Report to Leutnant Wenig. He will need you on damage control. Max, give me a course for the British airfield." Both officers saluted and went their separate ways. It took Max only moments to check his charts and give a new course, "Steer 055 degrees, sir. Target is approximately fifty kilometers northeast."

"Very well. Quartermaster steer 055."

The quartermaster repeated the order and both helmsmen acknowledged it. The distance to the enemy blimp field was short and things happened quickly. The two extra gunners moved forward one to each side of the forward control room. They slid open large windows and quickly mounted their MG 15s. The captain gave orders and the Zeppelin nosed down. They were sinking quickly as Max came forward to stand near the captain. He announced, "We will attack the airfield at 800 meters. We will approach from the south. Leutnant Wenig has saved a half dozen bombs and I intend to bomb the blimp hangars and shoot up any blimps moored in the open. Everyone keep your eyes open and call out any blimp sightings." There were excited nods. The captain then turned to Max, "Stand by the starboard gun. Direct its fire as needed." Max nodded his acknowledgement and moved over behind the gunner.

Leveling off at the lower altitude, the control car's occupants could now make out buildings, fields and orchards on the ground below. Looking at his watch Max realized that sunrise was just minutes away. They passed over a series of low hills and suddenly the helmsman in the nose of the car sang out, "Airfield in sight! Just over that next rise."

The captain and Max both trained their binoculars forward and seconds later Max sighted a huge square structure in the middle of acres of open ground. Smaller structures appeared and Max caught sight of a British flag waving from a tall pole. The captain ordered, "Steer for that hangar." He then moved to the bulkhead and picked up the intercom handset. As they flew low toward the expanse of the large airfield Max caught sight of another huge hangar on the far side of the field. It was end on to them. He focused on it but was distracted by a call of, "Blimps! Moored to port, on the other side of the hangar!"

Max turned and refocused. Sure enough, two blimps moored to short masts had come into sight as they neared the hangar .The huge bulk of the structure had shielded them from view as they approached. They were closing on the hangar at 80 kph. It grew in the view screen and Max heard the captain calling out quietly, "Steady. One minute"

Max spoke quietly to the gunner next to him, "After the hangar we'll steer for the blimps. Take the one on the right."

"Jawohl, Herr Leutnant."

The hangar filled the lower port and the captain spoke into the intercom, "Drop now." He then hung up and called out, "Port 20 degrees, Stand by to fire."

The gunner grabbed the charging handle on the side of his weapon and yanked it back and let go. He then pulled it to his shoulder and leaned forward. The Zeppelin came around slowly to port. As it did Max could clearly hear the distant bang of explosions somewhere behind them. No one looked back. Everyone was focused on the targets ahead. The gunner angled his gun forward along the side of the car. The captain, called out, "Steady...Steady...Fire!" The gunner in front of Max was ready and opened up with along burst. The tracers reached out and seemed to float gracefully in a stream toward the enemy. They were joined by other tracer streams from forward in the hull above them. The tracers arced out and the enemy airships seemed to absorb them effortlessly into their large gray, teardrop shaped envelopes. Max winced. He had again forgotten to put in his ear plugs. One of these days he would manage to get that right. The blimps were certainly not small targets at over eighty meters in length filled with tens of thousands of cubic feet of helium so Max didn't expect the balloon to collapse instantly. Still firing in long bursts he figured the gunner had put most of the belt of 8 mm bullets into the blimp. His gun clicked on empty and he immediately pulled the empty saddle drum loose and replaced it with a fresh one.

Reloaded, he pulled the weapon to his shoulder but Max put out a hand and said, "Save it for the next pass." The gun across from them had fallen silent as well. They were passing the two moored airships and the captain gave commands to turn the ship. They sailed forward and gradually began to come around. Now north of the hangar Max looked back and could see they had hit it hard. Part of the roof was collapsed and smoke spiraled up from the huge hole. The two blimps were visibly collapsing; the huge envelopes folding in on themselves and sagging towards the ground. Max nodded to himself, another pass would not be needed. The intercom buzzed and the captain answered it, "Bridge…Where? Thank you."

He hung up and stepped back to the port side training his binoculars and calling out, "Enemy Zeppelin on the other side of that far hangar. Hard a port. Gunners standby." Surprised Max turned. Sure enough emerging from the far end of the other hangar was a huge silvery shape. Their view of it had been blocked by the hangar on their approach from the south. The Zeppelin was coming slowly around in that direction. Max could feel the sudden tension of the bridge crew. As he focused on the new enemy he felt his heart beat faster. It was a full-sized airship. The nose and forward half of the ship had cleared the hangar doors and Max could see it was being pulled out by at least a hundred ground crewmen tugging on the mooring ropes. Worst of all Max recognized the unmistakable shape. The sharply pointed bow and smooth unbroken arc of the 230 meter hull identified her as one of the new R 80 class ships, the most advanced airships flown by the British.

They were over two kilometers distant but even at that range Max could see propellers turning on the sides of the ship. As it cleared the hangar he knew it was just moments from launching. Max called out, "Herr Kapitan, she is manned and her engines are turning."

The captain was lifting the intercom, "Peter, enemy Zeppelin just leaving the hangar. We have to attack." There was a pause, "I wish we had some left too. We'll go in low. All hull guns to target the Zeppelin. The gunners here will target the ground crew." He hung up and called out, "Gunners, standby!" The gunner in front of Max charged his weapon.

Suddenly a stream of tracers arced upward in front of the control car.

Max realized that although they couldn't hear or see it there must be chaos on the airfield. The attack on the blimp hangar had alerted the base and their AA gunners were reaching their posts. Now it was going to get rough. Max could see clearly the hundreds of men pulling on the mooring lines of the enemy airship. They were attempting to turn the British airship into the very light wind. He could see propellers turning on the near side of the airship. The enemy airship would launch in seconds.

The Zeppelin was racing across the field at 120 kph. They were still a kilometer distant from the enemy when Trautloff gave the command to open fire. The gunner near Max opened up but almost immediately a burst of machine gun fire came through the starboard bulkhead and the gunner was hit. He yelled out, clutched his chest and fell into Max. Max eased him to the deck. He was alive but Max couldn't take the time to help him. He leaped for the gun. He could hear yelling around him but the voices seemed far away as he pulled the gun to his shoulder, lined up the sight and squeezed the trigger.

The enemy ship filled the forward windows. Max's vision was narrowed and he couldn't see other lines of tracers converging on the enemy. All he could see was the men tugging on the mooring lines. He walked his fire along the tarmac toward them. He couldn't hear the screams but he saw soldiers fall. He swiveled the gun left, then right firing controlled bursts into the enemy. Dropping the mooring lines, men scattered in all directions. The silver hull of the enemy filled the forward view. It appeared they would crash into the side of the huge ship but Max concentrated on his gun. As they closed to three hundred meters he could not see the ground crew below the car. He raised his sights and sent his last dozen bullets into the aft port engine nacelle. He could actually see the bullets strike the aluminum engine housing. Smoke suddenly began pouring from the stricken engine.

Suddenly they were sailing over the giant enemy. Max dropped the gun from his shoulder but hung on to it. He looked around. Someone had thrown a jacket over the dead gunner. Everyone else was at their stations concentrating. Through the ringing in his ears Max could hear the captain giving orders for the ship to climb. Max leaned outward and looked down and behind them. The enemy airship appeared to be drifting low across the tarmac toward the edge of the airfield. He could see a propeller still turning but it didn't seem to be under much control.

As he watched, a gust of wind caught it and pivoted the ship until it was moving sideways. It reached some trees that brushed by its underbelly then the branches of one particularly tall tree caught the lower tail fin. The enemy pivoted around until the tail ripped free but this motion pulled the nose down to scrape through the tops of more trees.

Max was elated but he reminded himself to stay focused. He looked around for more ammo drums but saw none. He jumped across the gunner's body and ran for the back of the control car as the captain ordered the Zeppelin around for another pass.

On the ground Corporal Morton of the Duke of Norfolk's Royal Horse artillery vaulted over the sand bagged emplacement, one hand on the parapet the other holding on his flat 'tin hat' helmet. Sergeant Watson glared at him and yelled, "We're glad you could join us, corporal!" Morton glanced around. Private Brooks was pulling a cardboard wrapped shell out of an ammunition box that he had clearly just pried open with a bayonet. The other six men of the gun crew were nowhere to be seen. The attack had caught most of the British still in their bunks. Morton had been answering a call of nature when the sirens had sounded so he was at least awake. He had pulled on a pair of pants and grabbed his helmet as the first explosion rattled the windows of the barracks. The other soldiers were still tumbling out of bed as he raced toward his action station.

Sergeant Watson yelled, "Set the fuse on that shell, Morton." Then the sergeant leapt into the gunner's seat and began furiously cranking the hand wheels that elevated and pointed the gun. Morton took the heavy 3" shell from Brooks and set it down carefully nose up and looked frantically around. There; he grabbed for the arming tool and placed it carefully on the nose of the shell and began turning it, "What range, sergeant?"

The sergeant looked across the airfield at the huge airship hovering over the northern perimeter. Even at that distance it was still enormous, "Uh, twenty-five hundred yards." Morton spun the tool around two more turns and stood up. Dropping the fuse setter he picked up the long shell and ran toward the gun. The falling breach block was down. He rammed the shell in then grabbed the handle and jerked the breech block upward with a clang. "Loaded," he yelled! As he turned toward private Brooks he reached in his pocket and pulled out his ear plugs. Stuffing one in each ear he grabbed for the next shell the private was unwrapping.

Sergeant Watson had the gun trained out now. The huge silver Zeppelin was too big a target to miss even at that range he thought as he stood up and grabbed the firing lanyard. He turned his head away as he yelled out, "Stand clear!" and jerked the lanyard.

Brooks and Morton ducked as the gun fired with a huge, "Blam!" The gun recoiled and dust kicked up all around the position. As Morton set the fuse on the next shell Private Brooks jumped up and ran to the gun. He jerked the breech block lever down and the still smoking brass shell ejected clear of the gun and bounced to the back of the gun pit with a "clang."

Sergeant Watson craned his head upwards and saw the shell they had fired burst behind and below the Zeppelin. "Damn," he yelled in frustration. How had they missed? "Set fuse at 2800 hundred yards!"

He cranked the elevation wheel up. Having quickly reset the shell, Morton ran to the gun with it as Private Brooks ran to the ammunition box for anther wrapped round. Morton shoved the shell home and jerked up the breech block, "Loaded!"

Sergeant Watson turned the wheels gently. The Zeppelin's aspect was changing and it seemed to be climbing. The nose was rapidly swinging away from them. He sighted carefully, stood up and yelled, "Stand clear!" then he pulled the lanyard.

As Max brushed past the captain he felt the control car shudder from an explosion. The captain called out, "Gunners standby. Engines to full. Elevators full up; climb to 1200 hundred meters!" Max ran aft past the radio room and the navigator's station to the aft gunner's position. The gunner there was just reaching into a bin and pulling out a drum of ammo. Seeing Max, the gunner tossed it under hand to Max who caught the heavy object and nodded his thanks. The gunner then reached for another as Max started forward again. He had just reached the radio room when the radio operator stood up with a message form in his hand. The radio man stepped to the door but hesitated to let Max pass. At that moment an apparent lightning bolt hit the control car. Everything lit up in flash bulb brightness for a moment as thunder battered Max's ears. A freight train then collided with him as someone hit him in the face with a club. His head smashed into something hard and blackness swept over him.

Max regained consciousness slowly. His head was pounding and he seemed paralyzed. He couldn't move his arms or legs. He could see nothing out of his left eye and what he could see out of his right seemed twisted. The air was filled with dust and other debris. He could tell because he had dust in his mouth. He spit to clear it and a piece of paper plastered itself to his face. He shook his head and swore. This was a mistake because it felt like his head would fall off but the paper fluttered clear and suddenly he could see out of his right eye. Strangely, everything was quiet; silent as if he was watching a silent movie. He was lying on the deck. Max felt a weight lifted off him and suddenly he could move his arms. He pushed himself up and was face to face with someone he knew. He couldn't name him but he knew the face from somewhere.

The face was speaking. Max could see his lips moving but he could not hear anything except the ringing in his head. The young face reached out two arms, grasped Max's shoulders and shook him violently, "Herr Leutnant! Herr Leutnant!"

Suddenly Max could hear again. Engine noise and explosions filled the control car corridor. Wind rushed through and whipped bits of debris into this face. He realized he was down on the deck with the rear gunner crouched over him. The concerned look on the gunner's face worried him more than anything. "What happened," he gasped out?

"We were hit. The captain ..."

Max tried to push himself up, "Help me up. Where's the captain? How bad are we hit?"

The gunner grabbed Max under one arm and helped him up until he was leaning against the bulkhead, "Are you all right?"

Max shrugged his arm angrily, "Of course I'm all right. Where's the captain?"

"Forward. He's hurt badly." Concerned Max turned and attempted to run forward. He nearly fell but the gunner caught him again and helped him forward to the bridge. At that moment the whole Zeppelin shook violently. The gunner let go of Max's arm and said, "What was that?"

Supporting himself with a hand on one bulkhead Max ignored the question shocked by the destruction around him. With the exception of the curved Plexiglas at the front of the car every window had been blown out. Wind whipped through the bridge from seemingly all angles. The forward helmsman was on his feet desperately jerking the rudder wheel to and fro. It wasn't moving much at all. The port side gunner had been decapitated. His body sprawled in a tangled mess with the quartermaster's body on the deck. The elevator helmsman was crouched next to the captain who was down on the deck, his face covered in blood. More blood stained both legs of his uniform.

Max grabbed the gunner and yelled in his ear, "Get some help in here!" He then tried to reach the captain. It was harder than it looked. He was still unsteady and had no idea how bad he was hurt. Also he was attempting to walk uphill. Seconds later he dropped to one knee next to the captain. He grabbed a bloody cloth out of the helmsman's hand and yelled, "The nose is climbing. You have to level us off!" The man nodded grimly and pulled himself toward the elevator wheel. Max wiped gently at the captain's head. He was bleeding profusely from a large wound on the side of the head. Every time Max wiped blood away the wound immediately refilled with blood. Max gulped and tried to steady his stomach; he could see white bone. He then pressed the cloth firmly to the wound and sent up a silent prayer

The gunner appeared beside him and yelled, "The medic is on the way; the First officer too."

Max grabbed the man's hand and yelled, "Press here!"

Swaying slightly Max stood up carefully as the gunner took his place next to the captain. The deck was tilted down aft nearly fifteen degrees. The elevator helmsman spun the wheel all the way to the left until it stopped. He held it there and looked over his shoulder, a panicked look on his face, "Full down elevator, sir! But she's still sinking!"

Max moved toward him as the forward helmsman yelled out, "The rudder is jammed! I have no control!"

Max cursed and wiped at his left eye. He still couldn't see out of it. Staggering to the ballast control panel he squinted at it blurrily. His head was throbbing as he scanned the two parallel rows of white lit buttons. He stabbed hard at the two on the far right; one above the other and held them down. The lights flickered out. He glanced over at the elevator helmsman who was still holding the wheel at its stop. Dumping hundreds of liters of ballast hadn't helped. He cursed and pushed the next two buttons and held them. More ballast poured out of the aft bladders. At that moment the first officer lid down the ladder into the control car. He stared around in shock, "What the ..." Max turned and said, "We took a shell close aboard." He brushed at his eye and added, "I don't know why we're sinking...and the controls are jammed." Wenig stepped up to Max and grabbed his arm, "Are you all right?"

"Yes! Yes, I'm fine."

"Max your face is covered in blood."

Surprised Max wiped a hand on his face and looked at it. It came away bloody. Wenig grabbed his arm, "Max! Listen to me! I think we were hit aft. I need you to find out how bad we're damaged. Can you do that for me?"

Max wiped his hands repeatedly across his eyes and said, "Yes. I'm okay." He turned and grabbed a rung of the ladder.

It seemed like a very long climb but Max eventually reached the catwalk in the hull. Crewmen were running forward. He breathed deeply and started down the sloping catwalk. Yelling, "Make way!" he staggered aft. A hundred meters further and he realized that it was much brighter on the catwalk than it should have been. The tail area was open to the air. He finally reached cell twelve. Crewmen were swarming around it slapping patches on the huge gas cell. Others were climbing access ladders to reach its upper regions. Just ahead and above he could see cell thirteen was visibly hanging in its netting. Further aft he could see the lower part of cell fourteen was shredded, so was the outer hull fabric around it. Sunlight streamed in from the large tears in the hull.

On the catwalk Ernst was crouched on hands and knees peering down under the catwalk into the framework of the lower fin. Max dropped to his knees next to him. He had to yell over the wind and engine noise washing over them, "What happened?"

Not looking up Ernst yelled back, "A shell exploded below the fin. It shredded the two aft cells. It looks like there's a lot of damage down there." Max leaned forward and down next to the young officer. Most of the fabric covering had been torn off the lower fin. Max could see the ground clearly less than a thousand meters below. He saw instantly the Ernst was correct. He could see that some of the duralumin girders were twisted or actually parted from each other. He yelled, "The rudder is jammed! Can you see anything?" Ernst sat up and shook his head, "The rudder cables must be… What happened to you?"

"I'm fine. Ernst, we have to lighten the ship. Get every man not patching the cells to move forward. Dump any excess weight back here. The aft guns are heavy; send somebody up there to dump them over the side." Ernst nodded and asked, "What are you going to do?"

Max swung a leg over the catwalk's edge and yelled, "I've got to go down there and clear the rudder or we aren't going to make it. We're out of control." He found footing on a girder and swung his other leg over the catwalk's edge. Ernst hesitated for a moment then nodded. Jumping up he

"Get some help in here!"

moved aft down the catwalk.

Max had plenty of light in what should have been the darkened fin. Keeping his sight focused on the girders and not looking down he sidestepped to a large vertical girder. This was one of the cruciform girders that ran all the way up through the ship, through the upper fin, and crossed the horizontal girder that supported the large horizontal stabilizers. Three of these cross girders gave the tail tremendous strength. He worked his way around it and toward the second cruciform girder. Reaching that he lowered himself down a meter to rest on a lower horizontal duralumin girder running aft. Crouching down he looked around until he found the black control cable running aft. Ducking under a girder he began to crawl along a horizontal girder until he reached the cable. A hard tug on the cable confirmed Ernst's thought. The cable was taut and did not move. It must be pinched somewhere.

It had to be aft. Max turned to parallel the cable and crawled aft along the swaying girders. Going was slow. The air was swirling around him. Glancing down he could see sheered girders dangling and swaying near what should have been the lowest part of the tail. Below that he could see far below a field of crops. He could clearly see two human figures in the middle of the field staring up at the giant airship drifting overhead. Max resisted a mad urge to wave at them. As he reached a new cross girder he put his hand down on it and pushed forward. As he did the girder suddenly gave off a loud screech and sagged downward. As he tipped forward, Max grabbed at anything he could to brake himself. He grabbed a vertical strut and it tore loose in his hand with a screech. He pitched face forward off the girder with a yell.

Ernst reached the tail position. It was open to the air. The shell explosion had ripped large rents in the fabric covering. The wind from their speed had torn these rents into huge holes. Fabric that had not ripped away flapped from the tail cone. Ernst climbed up into the port position. The gunner was nowhere to be seen but there was blood all around the gun. As Ernst flipped open the breech of the gun and pulled the belt of 20 mm shells from it, he hoped the gunner had not been thrown or fallen out of the open port. Ernst fed the belt out the port and let it go. He disconnected the ammo box from the gun's side and tossed it after the belt. He then grabbed the gun's locking handle spun it around three times until it cleared the threads and yanked it from the mount to hang alongside the gun.

The 20 mm cannon was heavy; weighing nearly 40 kgs but fortunately Ernst didn't have to lift it very far. He simply levered it up out of its mount and tipped it forward and out of the port. He jerked his head back just in time to avoid being hit by the breech as it flipped up and outward. Ducking under the heavy tail girder assembly he quickly moved to the starboard mount and repeated this procedure. He climbed down and found two ammunition cans containing 20 mm ammo. He quickly dragged them to the edge of the catwalk and shoved them over. They clanged off two girders as they disappeared from sight. Satisfied he had dumped well over 150 kgs overboard he smiled as he sprinted back down the cat walk to Max.

As Max slid head first down the sloping girder he made a wild grab with his hands. His right hand got a good grip on a horizontal girder that seemed solid. He added his left arm and swung there for a moment the cold wind blowing across his face and up his pant legs. Finally he pulled himself up chest high on the girder and levered a leg up. He lay on the girder for a moment reflecting on what a long drop it was to the African plain before he resumed crawling toward the rear of the fin.

Moments later he saw the problem. A horizontal girder had been torn loose by the explosion and it was pinned against another girder. Between the two the black rudder cable could be seen. He was attempting to pull the girders apart a minute later when he heard Ernst's shouted voice, "Max! Did you find the problem?"

"Yes, but I need something to cut the cable. It's pinned and won't come clear."

"I'll find something…hold on."

Max laid his head on the girder and closed his eyes. The shock of getting hit was wearing off; his head was throbbing and his neck was rapidly stiffening up."

Minutes later Ernst was back. He crawled forward and passed Max a pair of bolt cutters. Max nodded his thanks. He hadn't even realized they had one on board. Wriggling around he crawled aft to where he could reach the pinned cable. The girder he was lying on creaked ominously but seemed to be holding. Reaching out the length of his arms he couldn't quite get the jaws of the cutters around the cable. Grumbling Max inched forward another foot. There was a screech and the girder he was laying on suddenly dropped 10 cm. Max gulped. Looking down he saw nothing but twisted and broken girders below him. If he slipped this time there would be nothing to grab onto. Focusing Max fitted the jaws of the cutter around the cable on the aft side of the girder. Shifting his grip he grabbed the handles and squeezed them as hard as he could. The cable snapped. The girder screeched and dropped downward. Max dropped the cutters and they fell, hitting a broken girder end before falling clear of the ship. Max slid forward his arms flailing and then something grabbed his ankle. He hung there for a moment then the hands on his ankle began pulling him back up the now angled girder.

Moments later Max and Ernst lay side by side on the cat walk both breathing hard. The two officers then pushed themselves to their feet. Max clapped the younger man on the shoulder, "Thanks, Ernst. It was a long drop back there."

Ernst smiled weakly, "We're running kind of short of officers today. Figured we might need you."

Max laughed and winced from the pain that caused, "Take charge up here. Try to lighten the ship if you can. Get rid of anything you can, and get everybody forward as soon as you get cell twelve patched up. I'll go report to Peter." Max turned and trotted forward holding a hand to his forehead.

Moments later he reached the control car ladder but had to stand aside as several men worked to pull the captain up the ladder. Now strapped to a stretcher he looked bad to Max's eye once he was lowered to the catwalk. The captain was very pale. His head was bandaged. His trousers had been cut away and his legs were covered in bandages. Once the ladder was clear Max dropped down and saluted Leutnant Wenig, "Sir, the rudder cable was pinched by wreckage. I cut it clear. Do you have helm control?"

Wenig nodded, "After a fashion. All we have is the upper rudder. The lower is flopping around loose. It's adding drag, but at least we can steer now. What happened back there?"

"It looked like a shell exploded just below the tail. The lower fin covering is shredded. There's a lot of structural damage too. We're lucky that tail hasn't fallen off. The shell tore up cells thirteen and fourteen. Ernst has a crew trying to save the gas in twelve. He's also lightening the ship aft. How's the captain?"

Wenig looked grim, "Bad. A concussion; and probably worse. Right now we've got to figure how to get him home. Can you find out where we are?"

"I'll try." Max moved carefully though the battered control car. There was a large hole in the lower radio room with light and air streaming through into the room. As he passed he saw the radio had been riddled with shrapnel. Max gulped. If the radio operator hadn't stood up at that exact moment Max would probably be dead. The unlucky operator's body had shielded Max from the worst of the blast.

The navigator's station was a mess. It took several minutes for Max to find the right charts amongst the paper blowing around the control car. The wind swirled through the car so that Max had to weight the map down on his table. He finally had a rough location plotted when Wenig leaned in, "Any news?"

Max pointed, "We're about here; southwest of Paarl. What's our course?"

"Southeast."

Max glanced at the chart, "That should bring us to the coast northeast of Cape Agulhas in uh…what's our speed?"

"We're doing about 120 kph. I've got the two aft engines at full power trying to keep the tail up but we're still heavy back there. I've dropped all the aft and amidships ballast. I'm keeping the forward ballast for emergencies."

Max looked at his watch; the crystal was shattered and the hands were bent, "What time is it?" Wenig told him.

"Then we should reach the coast in a little over an hour. It's going to be a warm day. That should give us some lift."

Wenig agreed, "Yes, but what are we going to do tonight when it cools off? I can keep her in the air like this for a while but lift is compromised and ballast is running low." He hesitated for a moment before dropping his voice until only Max could hear, "It's a long way home, Max. It's going to be a tough run back."

Max started to reply but was cut off by a noise from the bridge forward. The two officers moved forward to meet Brandel who had slid down the ladder into the car. He looked around silently for a moment then shouted to be heard over the wind whistling through the control car, "Where's the captain?"

Wenig answered, "He's badly wounded, I'm afraid. What's the status up top?" Ernst shook his head and answered, "We've got number twelve patched up. Numbers thirteen and fourteen are hopeless. Fortunately, they are smaller than the other cells. All crew has been moved forward of frame seven. We've lightened ship but are still looking for more things to get rid of. I came to ask if you want to jettison the glider?"

Max spoke up, "It's several hundred kilos."

Wenig thought for a moment then shook his head, "No. We keep it for now. Right now let's try to stabilize this thing and get north. The Tommies are alerted now. They'll be looking for us if they have any blimps left. I hope that Zeppelin was the only one operating this far south. If we run into another one, it'll be us on the receiving end of the club."

Wenig quickly organized the damaged ship. With the control car damaged and possibly unsafe, Wenig ordered it emptied except for an officer and the two helmsmen. Crewmen quickly patched canvas over the shattered windows. This cut visibility except directly ahead but it also cut down on the wind blowing through the car. Max finally visited the medic to have his head looked at. He had a nasty cut over his left eye; probably from being struck by the ammo drum he had been carrying, that took more than a few stitches to close. He also had a big lump on the back of his head from being slammed into the bulkhead. The medic told him he was probably slightly concussed and should rest. Max ignored him and went about his duties.

Once the Zeppelin reached the sea they turned east to parallel the coast. They were flying tail down at less than 1000 meters. It was high summer at this latitude and the day was clear and warm. Soon the enormous hull began to absorb heat from the sun and the helium in its cells began to expand. This had the effect of giving more lift. Gradually the Zeppelin began to climb. Normally a Captain would vent helium to maintain altitude. When the ship later cooled at night, he would then drop ballast to again maintain altitude. Unfortunately L-107 had little helium or ballast to spare. Wenig decided to let the ship rise naturally and save what gas and ballast he could.

Max spent the morning in the hull of the ship supervising repairs. There were many small tears in the outer hull covering. These were patched as well as possible. The crew continued to jettison anything they could spare. Small arms, bedding, clothing; everything that could be spared went over the side. He was checking fuel levels when Ernst found him, "Peter wants us in the control car, Max."

Max nodded and followed Ernst forward. Minutes later all three officers were huddled at the aft gunner's station in the damaged control car. Wenig looked sober, "I just spoke to the medic. The captain's in bad shape. He needs to get to a hospital soon or he's not going to make it." The others said nothing. Wenig continued, "I've got an idea. It's dangerous but I think it's his only chance. And, it might help the rest of us as well." He paused and turned to Ernst. "Can you strip the guns and radio out of the glider so that it can hold two people again?"

Surprised, Ernst hesitated for a moment before answering, "Sure. We can do that with a little work. What's your plan?"

"I'd like to have you fly the captain down to where he can get medical help."

Max frowned, "Where can we find a friendly hospital?"

Wenig replied, "Laurenco Marques."

Max was surprised for a moment then nodded, "That's a great idea and it's hardly off our course." Ernst looked surprised as well and then nodded. Wenig continued, "Right. And once down, Ernst can get word out through our consulate that we're damaged and returning. With no radio they have no idea what happened out here. How long until we can launch, Max?"

Max pushed past him to the navigator's table. Moments later he spoke, "We should be over Laurenco Marques about 2000 hour tonight, after dark."

Wenig thought a moment, "All right. You and Ernst get to work on the glider. I'm going to keep us off shore until we're north of Durban then we'll make straight for Laurenco Marques. If we can, I'd like to get us there by dark. Can you land that thing in the dark, Ernst?"

"Yes, I can land it in a park, a race track or even a football field but I need at least some illumination."

Max put in, "If they still work there might be a few flares left. But I think we can get there before nightfall."

"Good. That's the plan gentlemen." The three officers scattered to their duties. While the Zeppelin plowed north its tail still sagging low, Max and Ernst stripped the radio and twin 8 mm machine guns out of the glider. Ernst was startled for a second when he handed the first machine gun up to Max and he promptly slid it over the side of the glider and dropped it. Ernst thought about it and smiled, "Right, less weight." The other gun and the heavy radio soon followed. They then padded the rear seat area with blankets for the captain.

Under the hot southern sun the Zeppelin gradually gained height. By noon it was at two thousand meters. By four in the afternoon they were climbing toward three thousand meters. Wenig resisted the urge to drop any of his precious helium. Instead he watched the altimeter and safety valves carefully. The valves were set to vent helium automatically if the gas pressure grew too high. If they did there would be no way to control the helium loss.

In the afternoon they turned the ship north to cut across the northeastern corner of South Africa. This brought L-107 out over the ocean just east of the capital of Portuguese East Africa. It was now nearly seven o'clock in the evening and the sun was just above the western horizon. The officers of L-107 gathered in the drafty control car for a final briefing.

Wenig addressed Brandel, "Right now relations are pretty good with Portugal, Ernst. You should be accepted fairly well. Say nothing about our mission. Ask for the German consul and keep asking. When you see him brief him as we've agreed and ask him to get a message through to Dar Es Salaam. Be sure to give him a good report on what we saw at Simon's Town. And get the captain to a hospital as soon as you can."

The young leutnant, now dressed in leather flying jacket, gloves and leather helmet nodded, "Yes sir, hopefully someone will speak German or French."

Wenig reached out his hand, "You'll do fine. Good luck, Ernst."

Ernst shook the hand, "Thank you, sir." He stepped back and saluted, then turned and climbed the ladder into the hull with Max following. They made their way to the glider. Crewmen had loaded the captain into the rear cockpit. Ernst checked to make sure he was secure before he climbed into the forward cockpit. There he slipped on his goggles and nodded up at Max. Max bent over and slapped the young pilot on the shoulder and yelled out, "Good luck, Ernst. We'll see you at home."

Ernst smiled up at him. Max stepped back, held up three fingers, then two, then one. He then turned and waved at a crewman standing a few meters away. The crewman yanked down on a large handle and the glider dropped clear of the Zeppelin. Max then hustled away.

Back in the control room he found Wenig at the forward wind screen following the glider's progress with his binoculars. Max grabbed a set and did as well. Ernst had taken the glider down quickly. He was now circling over the city. The sun was slipping below the far horizon and it would soon be dark. As the two officers watched the glider circled to the west and lined up a long approach. The light-colored glider contrasted with the growing shadows on the darker ground and they clearly saw the glider slide across what appeared to be a large sports field and slow to a stop. Small figures could be seen running toward the aircraft.

With darkness, the cooler air contracted the helium in the Zeppelin's gas cells and gradually the great ship sank in altitude. Max was surprised when Wenig ordered the ship's course just east of north. Instead of heading out to sea they were crossing north over Portuguese territory. They would save many hours of flight. But there was a downside to the short cut. "What are the Portuguese going to say?" Max asked.

Wenig shrugged, "They may or may not lodge a protest. They know what's going on between us and the British. But as I told Ernst we're on pretty good terms with the Portuguese. Anyway, we have to risk it. We're low on helium and ballast and the damaged tail fin could tear away at any moment. I won't feel good again until we get this thing over German territory." Max nodded his agreement.

The great airship sailed on. Both officers spent the night in the control car with Max only leaving once to climb to the top of the Zeppelin for a star sighting. With a good chart fix he adjusted their course and they cruised over the lights of Beira before dawn the next morning. Beira was a small town and seemed very quiet. Both officers crossed their fingers and hoped that no one saw the Zeppelin cruise across the bay at just over a thousand meters.

Dawn brought scattered clouds rather than blue sky. They had passed back into the tropics during then night leaving the warm summer weather behind. The brief tropical wet season was once again ahead of them. Despite the overcast the day was warm and humid. As the air warmed the Zeppelin again gained height.

Just after noon, Wenig took a call on the intercom from somewhere in the hull. He hung up the handset and turned to Max, "There's something wrong with the number three engine. Go up and take a look, Max."

Max nodded and headed for the ladder. In the hull he made his way down the sloping main catwalk to the mid ship engines. He then climbed lateral steps to the big diesel engine. The noise made by the engine forced the chief machinist mate to shout in Max's ear, "Herr Leutnant, we're going to have to shut down the engine."

Max shouted back, "What's wrong?"

"Can you hear that whine? We're losing a bearing. We're grinding the heart out of the engines running them at full speed for this long."

Max listened for a moment but his ear wasn't attuned to the big engines like the chief's was, "Shut it down if you have to but we have to keep the other engines running full. They're the only thing keeping us in the air now. If we don't keep the two aft engines adjusted full downwards the tail is going to drop even lower."

The chief nodded grimly and saluted. Max left and reported back to the control room. Wenig looked unhappy, "How far to Lindi?"

Lindi was the closest German town in the southeast corner of the DOA. Max thought a moment, "We were about six or seven hours out but we're going to be later now if we lose one engine. It'll be dark by the time we get there."

Wenig was silent for a moment, "I don't want to try and land this beast after dark. Even if we could radio ahead for lights I'm not sure they would turn them on. It would make a great target for any British airships or warships offshore." He thought a moment, "Maybe we should slow up and try for the Rufiji. We could then land in the morning."

Max agreed, "That is if we can stay in the air that long."

"We'll make it. Give us a new course. Speed 100 kph."

Max headed for his charts.

The weather continued warm and humid. Thunderstorms loomed close to the northeast. The first rains squalls hit them at 1500. They had gained altitude and were at 2300 meters when the rain began. Fortunately there was not much wind. The temperature drop caused by the rain plus the weight of the water clinging to the huge hull forced the Zeppelin lower. They soon passed out of the squall and the airstream quickly dried them. They began to climb again until the next rain squall broke over them. This pattern was repeated all afternoon.

The air grew more turbulent and the ship began to be tossed about. The helmsmen did their best but they had little control. The rudder was slow to respond and when the elevator was moved the tail dropped even more. Max spent most of the afternoon in the hull watching how the hull was taking the weather and checking on the damaged tail fin. He could hear the great ship groan as it flexed. The huge rings that supported the gas cells were all intact but several of the wires that stabilized the aft rings had snapped when they had been hit. He was worried about losing more wires as the ship flexed in the rough weather.

Wenig ordered a course change westward trying to avoid the worst of the weather but it did not seem to help. The afternoon wore on. The crew was tired. Regular meals weren't served. The crew grabbed what food they could eat at their stations while they worked.

It was after dark, and Max was relieving Wenig in the control car so the First officer could get something to eat, when they were hit by the first of a series of massive gusts. They were approaching a massive, unseen thunderstorm cell. The first gust hit them and drove the whole ship sideways. Before the helmsman could regain control the ship tilted upward and they were swept upwards by a powerful torrent of wind. Max nearly fell as he was thrown aft but managed to catch a control panel. His legs dangling in air Max guessed their up angle at over forty degrees. He had no idea how far they were thrown upwards but it seemed like he hung there forever. The helmsmen hung desperately to their control wheels looking terrified. Wenig meanwhile had been thrown into a rear corner of the bridge and was clawing himself upward toward the intercom. Reaching it he yelled something Max couldn't hear because of the wind roaring through the car. The temporary canvas covering the shattered windows had been sucked out into the darkness.

Finally the ship slowed and remarkably they leveled out. For a few moments they seemed to hang suspended on an even keel rocking back and forth. Regaining his feet Max staggered to Wenig and yelled, "We must have slipped out of the up draft. We've got to head west and get out of this. The ship can't take this kind of strain." Wenig nodded and yelled commands at the helmsmen. Max turned and was thrown forward onto his face as the nose of the Zeppelin plunged downwards as the ship was caught in a sudden downward gust. Crawling toward a bulkhead Max managed to pull himself to his feet and cling to a control panel. Wenig staggered to the elevator control and helped the helmsmen spin the wheel full up. Max pulled himself to the altimeter and was shocked to see how fast the arrow was spinning counter clockwise. He didn't know how high they had been lifted but they were now passing swiftly downwards past 3500 meters.

He watched fascinated as the arrow spun around. 3000 meters. 2800 meters. 2600 meters. They were traveling downwards at over 500 meters per minute. They reached 2000 meters and Max could feel the nose coming up. The thicker air was slowing them slightly but they were still sinking too fast. Wenig screamed over the wind whistling through the cabin, "What's the altitude?"

"Passing 2000 meters!"

Still holding on to the elevator wheel Wenig yelled, "We have to slow the ship or it'll break apart! Drop the ballast! All of it!"

Max didn't bother to nod. He turned and pulled himself toward the ballast panel. Reaching it he stabbed at the remaining white lit buttons. Seconds passed as he continued dumping the remainder of the Zeppelin's precious ballast. The panel completely dark, Max turned forward. Wenig looked triumphantly over his shoulder, "Its working!"

Max then realized the nose of the ship was slowly coming up. Jumping to the altimeter he saw they were still descending but the arrow was unwinding more slowly. He yelled, "We're slowing!"

The Zeppelin continued descending but at a slower rate. The wind noise diminished as gradually they flew out of the storm cell. Wenig staggered over to Max and said, "I think we made it. What's the altitude?"

"750 meters but we're slowing. I don't know how low we're going to go."

"Nothing we can do about it now but pray." Max's eyes were glued to the dial. The arrow continued to slow and finally stabilized at 200 meters. He looked at Wenig who too was staring at the dial, "The tail has got be skimming the tree tops." Wenig simply nodded. A moment later he spoke to the helmsmen. "Hold this course west." He then lowered his voice and said to Max, "I want to go west and let the worst of these storms pass. Then we'll try to circle back to the east."

Max warned, "We can't go too far inland. If the land rises much we're going to be in the trees."

Wenig agreed, "We'll slow the ship as much as possible." Turning he called up the engine changes and then spoke to the helmsmen.

They spent the next several hours churning slowly west and eventually north. The violent turbulence had abated but they still flew through light rain showers and fought a crosswind out of the south. Max breathlessly craned his head out one of the shattered windows craning forward trying to spot high ground looming out of the darkness. The ship was very low. With no more ballast and flying tail low any high ground would be their doom.

Sometime after midnight the air settled down. At that point Wenig ordered the ship around to the east northeast. It was only a guess but Max figured that course would take them somewhere toward the Rufiji River delta.

By the time the sky began to lighten Max could barely keep his eyes open. The only thing that kept him awake was the fresh airstream in his face and his fear that they would fly into some kind of obstacle.

There was no true dawn just a lightening of the gloom. The sky was overcast but the winds and rain had subsided somewhat. Wening called Max to the navigator's table, "Where do you think we are?" Max tried to figure the time and distance in his head but his mind seemed fogged. Finally he said, "I'm sure we're over German territory somewhere. I'd have to guess we're somewhere southwest of the Rfiji but where exactly I can't say without a firm navigation fix."

Wenig nodded, "Then let's keep a watch for landmarks." It was light enough for heavy forest just beneath them to be seen clearly. Both officers kept a sharp eye out for villages, streams or anything to help give their location. Nothing but featureless trees sailed under their keel. Suddenly the jungle came to end and L-107 sailed out over a gray choppy surf above the Indian Ocean. Max smiled broadly. Wenig brought the ship around north to follow the coast.

Less than an hour later the delta of the Rufiji came into view.

Their landing was terrifying for Max. With no altitude and the tail hanging much lower than the control car he had no idea how they could bring the ship down safely. Wenig handled the job masterfully. As they neared the airfield north of the main naval base he ordered the engines to full up for lift and let the ship drift toward the mooring mast. Hundreds of sailors filled the field below to watch the ship drift in. When he dropped the landing lines they were hastily grabbed by sailors and the ship was pulled in toward the mast. With the mooring line attached to the mast it reeled the nose toward the mooring cup. Wenig went idle on the forward engines and to bring the nose down as it was reeled toward the mast. Max felt the jar as the nose locked into the mooring mast cup and the ship steadied. Slowly the tail sank downward. It hit the ground almost gently. Here was a huge screech as duralumin girders crunched and the tail settled to the ground. There was afinal metallic screech as the tail fin folded in on itself and the tail settled to the tarmac.

Wenig called the chief engineer in the hull and ordered him to secure the engines. He then turned to Max as the giant ship fell silent, "I guess we made it." Max smiled weakly, "Good landing."

Wenig's response was cut off by hammering on the outside access hatch in the rear of the car.

"Better get that hatch open, Max. We've got to get the wounded off."
"Yes, sir."

The next day Max was supervising a crew of sailors building a temporary scaffold around the tail of L-107. Wenig stood nearby speaking with the base facilities officer. The plan was to build a structure to support the tail of the airship so they could begin assessing the damage. Other crewman and base mechanics swarmed around the battered control car.

Max looked around as he heard a powerful diesel engine. A large black staff car flying an admiral's pennant was approaching fast. He turned and hustled over next to Wenig as the car braked to a stop ten meters away. A door opened and out popped a young leutnant who hurried around to open the other rear door. From out of the car emerged Admiral Schall commander of all naval forces in the colony.

Wenig and Max stiffened to attention as did every enlisted man in sight. The admiral was trim, gray haired officer of perhaps fifty years. He returned their salutes and spoke, "Leutnant Wenig; Leutnant Von Clausen. Welcome home."

Wenig replied, "Thank you, sir." Max added his thanks as well. The Admiral called, "Stand at ease, men." He then stepped forward and shook both of the officer's hands, "Let me congratulate you both on bringing your ship in safely. It was an extraordinary feat of airmanship." Max was surprised but managed to stutter out another 'Thank you, sir.'

The admiral continued, "You men did fine job out there. The information and film you brought back has been invaluable to our defense. I want you to know that I've recommended you both for decorations." He raised his voice, "In fact I've cited the whole crew for outstanding performance."

Wenig nodded his thanks, "That's gratifying, sir. But have you heard anything about the captain and Leutnant Brandel?"

"We have. Captain Trautloff was successfully operated on and is safely in a Portuguese hospital. He is to be evacuated back to Germany as soon as he can be moved safely."

"And Leutnant Brandel, sir" Max asked?

"Ah, that's a little more difficult. The British have requested he be turned over to them as a war criminal, failing that they want him permanently interned by the Portuguese."

Max was appalled and his emotion must have shown on his face because the Admiral smiled indulgently at him, "That kind of thing is to be expected, son. What will probably happen is the Portuguese authorities will make some soothing neutral noises and then quietly release him in a few weeks or months when interest dies down. That's the way things usually work out in these situations."

Relieved, Max nodded as the Admiral continued, "Berlin will be sending some engineers out, hopefully soon, to survey the damage and plan repairs. He turned to Wenig, "Do you have everything you need Leutnant?"

Wenig nodded, "For the time being, sir."

"Good. Because I have plans for Von Clausen here." He turned back to Max, "L-139's first officer was wounded by flak over Kamerun a few days ago. I'm assigning you temporarily to Korvetten Kapitan Priller until his first officer can fly again."

Surprised Max could only agree, "Of course, sir."

"Good. The British are planning something big soon and we'll need every available man."

Nine days later Max leaned forward and focused his binoculars over the side of L-139's cloud car as a flare burst in brilliant light below him. On the darkened ocean below the bright light threw several British warships into stark relief. Above him in the clouds L-139 circled slowly over the British squadron at 3300 hundred meters. The air was cold at 700 meters below the ship and Max pulled his leather jacket closer around him. Both of the remaining German Zeppelins had been tracking the British fleet north for three days. The British ships were in two squadrons now pushing into the Mozambique Channel. The forward group over which L-139 was circling consisted of two British Battleships, *Rodney and Renown* it was thought, plus two heavy cruisers all encircled by six patrolling destroyers.

Several kilometers behind, a group transports and two large troopships escorted by another five destroyers followed. The British has somehow managed to scrounge up two blimps to fly anti-submarine patrol over the combined fleets as well. L-139 and L-102 had attacked the blimps at dawn. Unable to run, the blimps had taken shelter over the fleet's anti-aircraft guns. It had done them no good. Braving the flak the two Zeppelins had come in from above and quickly shot down the two blimps. The little airships were practically unarmed and been helpless. Max remembered clearly the three crew members jumping from their ships. All four parachutes opened and the crew descended toward the fleet. Max hoped they had been picked up.

L-139 had taken some minor damage from flak near misses but these were quickly patched and their surveillance continued. The two Zeppelins had shadowed the British force all day. Slipping in and out of the clouds and occasional rain squalls they had sent constant location reports updating Admiral Schall on the position of the British squadron. Captain Priller had briefed the crew that every available German ship in East African waters had been assembled and were closing from the north. They had been dropping flares over the British ships since sunset to illuminate the enemy as their own ships closed for a night attack.

Max felt himself tense as flashes lanced out from the enemy battleships below. He reached for the handset. Moments after he had lifted it to his ear Captain Priller answered, "Bridge."

"Enemy has opened fire to the north."

"Very well. Any sign of our forces?"

"No. Uh, wait one." Max lifted his binoculars and focused where he thought he had just seen something. Moments later, there were more rippling flashes in the distance. He spoke again into the handset, "Sir, I have gun flashes to the north. Our ships must have opened fire."

"Very well, report changes."

Max put down the handset and concentrated on the battle unfolding before him. The German ships attacking out of the darkness initially had the advantage firing on the illuminated British but this proved fleeting. The British cruisers fired star shells to illuminate the German ships. German gunnery was accurate and Max reported every hit on the British battleships but the 125, 150 and 203mm guns of the German cruisers didn't seem to do much damage to the heavily armored British battleships. They shrugged aside the cruiser shells and continued firing. To the north Max could see the huge white columns of water thrown up by British shells. Eventually he was appalled to see them score multiple hits on a German cruiser.

Soon the German ship fell out of line burning heavily amidships. About this time the accompanying German destroyers made a torpedo attack on the British. The six destroyers closed rapidly with the British line through heavy fire. Max saw one destroyer sail through the huge water spouts thrown up by the shells of a battleship to turn and fire a spread of torpedoes. Another was not so lucky and simply disappeared in a blinding explosion as a salvo of heavy shells found its magazines.

Although he couldn't tell for certain the other German destroyers must have fired their torpedoes because they soon turned away into the darkness, another ship burning fiercely. The British fire faltered as their ships all maneuvered to avoid the torpedoes but minutes later the British squadron had reformed in line ahead and their fire picked up once more.

Max picked up the handset to report the failure of the torpedo attack when something below caught his attention. Suddenly, white pillars of water had erupted against the sides of the British ships. Max realized instantly that they were torpedo explosions…but they were on the unengaged side of the British ships, the southern side opposite the German destroyers. The captain's voice rang in his ear, "Cloud Car, report." Max ignored the voice demanding his attention as he silently counted torpedo strikes; one, two , three, four, five… finally he found his voice and called out, "Torpedo strikes! Multiple torpedo strikes on the enemy! They are coming from the south, repeat the south."

There was the slightest pause before Captain Priller replied, "Good work, Leutnant. Continue reports." Max hung up the handset and refocused his binoculars on the ships below. He found himself nodding as he focused on a battleship that appeared to be slowing. From the angle of the strikes, the torpedoes could only have come from German U-boats. Naval High Command must have quietly brought U-boats to East African waters. That was why the Zeppelins had been ordered to destroy the enemy blimps that morning, and why the illumination of the British ships was so important. The sacrifice of the German surface ships had lured the British over a line of U-boats that had struck without warning.

Even now Max could see that the British had ceased fire. One of the battleships appeared to be turning south and increasing speed. The other battleship was definitely slowing and one of the British cruisers seemed to be dead in the water. Meanwhile British destroyers raced in all directions searching for the enemy U-boats.

Max turned his binoculars to the south. Illuminated by flares dropped by L-102, Max could see confusion among the second British squadron. Multiple ships were on fire. Explosions came to his ears and he could see white columns of water thrown in the air. The transports were also under U-boat attack

Max let out a long breath. It looked like the crisis had passed.

The tall windows of the wood paneled conference room were misted over from the cold outside. December had turned cold and snow was forecast for London. It looked to be a white Christmas. The gray haired First Sea Lord gave the multi-page report to a uniformed aide who carried it around the long conference table to the defense minister. Sober looking admirals and Generals sat in silence around the table.

The minister took the report and flipped through it, pausing only momentarily at each page. Near the end of the report he stopped and re-read a passage. He looked up at the First Sea Lord over the top of his metal framed eye glasses, "Is this casualty figure correct?"

There was a slight stir from among the officers. The First Sea Lord looked pained and cleared his throat before answering, "Not exactly, minister. The Germans claim to have rescued large numbers of our men. I'm hopeful that significant numbers of those 'Missing in Action' will be eventually returned to us."

The minister handed the report to his aide and spoke to the table at large, "Is there any way we can present this to the public as anything other than a major disaster?"

The silence that answered him was deafening. He looked accusingly at the First Sea Lord and asked forcefully, "And nothing could have been done to save *Rodney*?"

The First Sea Lord cleared his throat before answering, "Our forces successfully fought off additional U-boat attacks and believe they sank one. Flooding was stopped and she was under tow off Portuguese East Africa and out of trouble, so we thought, when bad weather ensued. In heavy weather *Rodney* broke her tow line and before the tugs could regain control she listed, took on water and capsized in less than an hour. Fortunately most of her crew had been evacuated and casualties were light."

The Minister drummed his fingers on the table for a moment before speaking, "All reports are to be classified until further notice...especially casualty reports. Is that clear, Gentlemen?" There were cautious nods around the table. The Minister stood and pulled his watch from its pocket. He flipped it open, checked the time and replaced it in his pocket, "I am due at 10 Downing Street within the hour. The Prime Minister wants to see this report but I'm afraid he has already decided to request a ceasefire from the Germans." There was a stir from the assembled officers before the minister continued, "I am told the King has sent a personal note to the Kaiser." The minister pushed back from the table and walked to the far end of the room followed by his aide and picked up his hat. He turned and nodded to the watching officers, "Good day, Gentlemen."

His aide opened the door for him and the Minister left without another look back. The door closed on the silent room. The First Sea Lord stood up and walked to the window, his back to the room. As he stared out he saw that it had started to snow.

Standing in the dim light of the enormous Zeppelin hangar at the Tabora airfield, Korvetten Kapitan Peter Wenig turned to his newly promoted first officer and asked, "When will the doping be finished?"

Nodding at the men brushing silver-colored coats of thick liquid onto the newly repaired fin of their airship L-107, Kapitan Leutnant Ernst Brandel replied, "The men will be finished this afternoon. We should give it at least twenty-four hours. We can do a test flight any time after that, Captain."

"Good the engineers are anxious to take it up and see if their new handiwork stands up."

"Those Zeppelin Works boys seem to have done a good job. I'm confident. Although, it won't be as exciting as your last flight." The young leutnant shook his head at the thought.

Wenig looked thoughtful, "We were lucky...oh, speaking of Max I got a letter from him on the last mail ship." He pulled an envelope out of his jacket pocket and handed it to the younger man. Ernst pulled a sheet of stationary from the open envelope as he moved toward the yawning hangar doors for more light. He read:

Peter, Hamburg, 3April

I hope this letter finds you well. I am sorry I haven't written lately but they keep us hopping here at the Weapons Testing Center. I wish I could tell you about some of the new projects we have going here but they would probably court martial me if I did. I can say that we will be bringing some great new weapons on line in the next year or two. Since Africa is a hot zone I wouldn't be surprised if we won't be doing some field testing out your way soon.

Speaking of testing, you said 107 would be ready for her test flight soon. I'm envious. Sometimes I wish I was still back there with you and the old crew. I haven't actually flown in the three months I've been here. It's all just designing and building prototypes and testing. Still, it's interesting work.

I took the train down to Berlin last weekend to have dinner with the captain and his wife. Frau Trautloff is a wonderful woman who really made me feel at home.

The captain is doing well. He's completely recovered and is chafing at his desk job. He may not be there for long though. He has been lobbying hard for a flying command and the rumor is that he's getting one of the new zeps.

I should close this letter and finish packing. I'm being sent on temporary duty to help set up the new testing range. The army has taken over some island in the Baltic and is turning it into a weapons test range. Supposedly for something new they're working on. The navy is also involved and I've been assigned to help set up things out there for a month or two.

Take care of the ship and tell Ernst to write more often. Both of you take care and watch out for the Tommies.

Regards,
Max

Ernst re-folded the letter as Wenig strolled up. The younger officer handed him the letter back and the two turned and left the hangar. As they walked across the airfield Ernst remarked, "Well, it seems like Max is having a lot of fun."

"Funny, he seems to think we're having all the fun."

"We will be, once we get the ship back in the air. I'm getting tired of repairs and inspections. So is the crew. They're hungry for some action.

"Now, Ernst you know that we have a cease fire with the Brits."

"Sure, but we had one last Fall and it didn't make any difference; I don't trust them."

"And we shouldn't. Once the ship's in the air again we'll be keeping a close eye on them. Although the Admiral did hint that he has some special work for us."

Ernst perked up, "Really, then why don't you buy your first officer a beer and tell him about it."

"As junior officer Herr Leutnant, I would think it would be more appropriate for you to be buying the drinks for your commanding officer."

Ernst smiled, "Jawohl, Herr Kapitan."

THE END

ABOUT OUR CREATORS

AUTHOR

GENE MOYERS - studied European and Medieval history at the University of Oregon. He is also a U.S. Army veteran. He worked in the high-tech industry for some time and ran a store front and internet hobby shop for several years. An avid military gamer and role player, his favorite game was *Daredevils* a pulp based roleplaying game set in the 1930s. His love affair with the 1930s and pulps in particular stem from his first time reading a *Shadow* novel as a boy. Although interested in writing since a teen he did not turn to serious writing until 2000.

He is the co-author of *GURPS Crusades* published by Steve Jackson Games. He has now written several stories for Airship 27 including stories published in *Ravenwood, The Purple Scar, The Domino Lady, Black Bat, The Phantom Detective,* and *The Legends of New Pulp Fiction.* He has also written a story for *Alternative Air Adventures* for Pro Se Publications and has been published in two Moonstone Books anthologies.

When not working on various new pulp projects he is busy writing horror adventures for his colonial swashbuckler or his occult investigator, the *Dream Master.* Gene currently lives in Beaverton Oregon with his wife and two lazy dogs.

INTERIOR ILLUSTRATIONS –

MIKE HARRIS - attended New York City's Stuyvesant High School ('79) where he studied writing under Frank McCourt, and School of Visual Arts, where he studied under Will Eisner, Harvey Kurtzman, Marshall Arisman, and Gil Stone; His influences included J. C. Leyendecker, Heinrich Kley, and Neal Adams.

Breaking into the industry in 1985, he worked as a fill-in artist on several Marvel Comics titles, such as *Web of Spider-Man, The 'Nam, Nomad,* and *Nova: Deathstorm.* Harris (with writer David Michelinie) co-created the Spider-Man enemies Chance and Foreigner, both in *Web of Spider-Man #15* (June 1986). Later, Mike contributed to *Punisher War Zone,* and *Punisher War Journal,* and illustrated the Marvel limited series *Cops: The Job, No Escape,* and *Dragon Strike.* During the 1980s, before becoming a Marvel Comics regular, Harris also freelanced for DC Comics (where he illustrated, among others, *All-Star Squadron*), Comico, Deluxe Comics, Eclipse Comics, Fantagraphics, First Comics, and Harris Publications. In the mid-1990s, Harris worked for Tekno Comix/Big Entertainment on such titles as *Lost Universe* and *Lady Justice*.

During this period he also did some G.I. Joe mini-comics, which were packaged with the toys; and illustrated a Magnus, Robot Fighter trading card for Valiant Comics. Leaving comic books in 1997, Mike moved on to the computer game and animation industries.

While working as a comic book artist, Harris enlisted in the New York Army National Guard as a Cavalry Scout, 19D, with the 1-101st Cavalry in 1986. He was selected to attend Officer Candidate School and was commissioned in 1988 as an Armored Cavalry officer. He continued to serve in the National Guard and Army Reserve while working as an illustrator from 1986 through 2004, and served on active duty from 2004-2016. He deployed to Iraq in support of Operation Iraqi Freedom from 2004-2005 and again in 2008 on Leaders' Reconnaissance missions in support of deploying units. He retired from the Army in 2016, at the rank of Leutnant colonel, after thirty years of active and reserve service. His awards include the Legion of Merit, the Meritorious Service Medal, Army Reserve Commendation Medal (four awards), the Army Achievement Medal, the New York State award for Support to Civil Authority, a Meritorious Unit Citation and a Superior Unit Citation.

Mike and his wife, Julie, have been married more than 15 years and have two children, Fiona and Lily.

COVER ARTIST -

BRIAN R. McCULLOCH - Born in Northern Oklahoma at seventeen Brian had a choice between Art School or Navy Bootcamp, the latter had better benefits. But at twenty two after separating from the military through a series of odd coincidences and questionable decisions he hound himself living in Mississippi and driving as often as possible to Wake Forest NC to attend every class Dru Blair and the Blair School of art had to offer.. Then through some dumb luck and being too stubborn to stop making pretty pictures he founded 214 Art Studios in Pensacola FL and continues creating art traditionally and digitally. https://214artstudios.com/

FOG OF TERROR

A hooded man suddenly appears on the streets of Akelton carrying a strange device strapped to his back. Affixed to it is a nozzle from which enveloping black fog spews forth quickly swallowing everything in its path; to include men, women and children. Just like that the city is thrown into panic as the mysterious villain begins popping up all over the city wielding his eerie weapon.

Realizing he is facing a supernatural threat, Captain Dan Griffin enlists the aid of the city's own gruesome crime fighter, the Purple Scar. The Scar—secretly plastic surgeon Doctor Miles Murdoch—with the aid of his nurse Dale Jordan and ally Tommy Pedlar is quickly on the hunt for the mastermind behind the fog of terror. For the first time in his vigilante career, the Purple Scar is battling an evil scientific genius whose purposes can only herald doom and bloodshed. It is a battle he cannot afford to lose.

THE PURPLE SCAR
VOLUME THREE
"The Black Fog"
BY GENE MOYERS

HORROR AND JUSTICE COLLIDE

AN AIRSHIP 27 PRODUCTION

AIRSHIP27HANGAR.COM

NEW PULP

PULP FICTION FOR A NEW GENERATION!